The Secret Life
of a Boarding School Brat

The Secret Life of a Boarding School Brat

AMY GORDON

Holiday House / New York

To the memory of Bob Eaton,
who was the original Silly Wizard

With thanks to Elena Tillman and Sarah Young
(They know why.)

Copyright © 2004 by Amy Gordon

All Rights Reserved

Pictograms by Heather Saunders

Printed in the United States of America

www.holidayhouse.com

First Edition

1 3 5 7 9 10 8 6 4 2

Library of Congress Cataloging-in-Publication Data

Gordon, Amy, 1949–

    The secret life of a boarding school brat / Amy Gordon.—1st ed.

      p. cm.

    Summary: Unhappy to be sent to boarding school after her parents' divorce and her father's remarriage, seventh-grader Lydia chronicles her experiences, secret feelings, and changing outlook about her situation in the diary that her grandmother gave her before she died.

    ISBN 0-8234-1779-4 (hardcover)

    [1. Boarding schools—Fiction. 2. Schools—Fiction. 3. Self-perception—Fiction. 4. Interpersonal relations—Fiction. 5. Divorce—Fiction. 6. Diaries—Fiction.] I. Title.

PZ7.G65Se 2004

[Fic]—dc22

2003056753

Monday, January 4, 1965

I, Lydia Rice, am an insomniac.

That's what Miss Hammer, the nurse at the Florence T. Pocket School for Girls, called me just now. She caught me prowling in the hall for the second night in a row. She said I had black circles under my eyes and that I was an insomniac, a person who can't sleep at night. She said, "Lydia Rice, you get right back in your room. If I catch you out here one more time, you will be in serious trouble."

I should have told her I hate boarding school and want to be home with Mom, but I can't. Someone might tell Mom, and then Mom would be upset. Dad-and-April would find out, and they'd be mad and say I'm not trying.

Now what? I can't wake up my roommate, Lacey. She just falls right back to sleep.

Gran gave me this diary for Christmas two years ago. I didn't think of writing in it until now. I guess I wasn't really old enough. Gran said it would feel as if I were writing to a friend, and I guess I had friends then so I didn't need to write. Gran also said it would be interesting to read when I'm older, but I think she was wrong about that. I am *not* going to want to read about this horrible old boarding school. I'm going to want to forget *everything* about it. But you know what? I do feel less lonely when I write in my diary.

Lacey's bedspread is pink. Her nightgown is pink. Her bathrobe is pink. She is from Atlanta, Georgia. She talks in a soft southern accent. She is tall the way I wish I could be, but she's so flimsy it seems as if she doesn't have any bones or muscles. Because she's from the South, she's always cold. I think she has water in her veins instead of blood.

The pink bathrobe was a Christmas present. Earlier I asked her if she minds being back at school. All she said was, "It's fine." I asked her what she did over vacation, and she said, "Not much." She didn't ask me what I did over vacation. I don't know why I can't ever have a conversation with my roommate.

I am wearing one of Gran's old work shirts over my pajamas. It smells like Hidden Lake. It has Jip's hair all over it. Jip was Gran's dog. I have a snapshot of him on my bureau.

How can Lacey be sleeping? How can she always do what she's supposed to do? She has room-study because she gets good grades. During study hall she sits at her desk, which is always neat, and gets all her homework done.

Now everything is quiet and still in the hallways of Pocket House. No radios and record players and no Whitney Brewer and Collie Baxter laughing like hyenas over stupid things. Now I am going out prowling again. Even if the halls are dark and creepy. I don't care. The Mad Prowler is afraid of nothing, ha-ha-ha-ha-ha!

Tuesday, January 5

Last night I ran up and down my hallway. I felt so free without anyone looking over my shoulder, telling me what to do. No sign of Miss Hammer. I think I'll be safe from now on by just waiting a little longer.

Later I got adventurous and decided to go down to the first floor. Every time I go down the old wooden Pocket stairs, I think of all the feet that have gone before mine—all the girls enslaved by the Pocket School for centuries—well, maybe not centuries, but a lot of years. Were they homesick, too? I feel homesickness for Mom all the way down to my toes.

The first floor has the boarders' dining room, and sitting rooms, and Mr. Wing's office. He is our beloved (heh-heh) headmaster. Mr. Wing reminds me of a blood-hound with saggy cheeks. I don't think he really runs the school. I think the real bosses are Miss Sparring, who is head of boarding, and Mr. O'Hare, who is dean of students. Miss Sparring reminds me of a dead tree. She is spiky and scary, and she will never grow leaves again. Mr. O'Hare reminds me of a rabbit. He has a lot of big teeth. Mr. O'*Hare*, get it? We should call him Mr. O'*Rabbit*.

I went into the sitting room where the teachers smoke after meals. It has fancy chairs and couches, an Oriental carpet, and a large portrait of Miss Pocket. She is wearing a satiny blue dress and sitting up very straight with her hands folded in her lap. She reminds me of Gran—I mean, I think she is the kind of person who makes me feel shy at first, but then when you get to know her, you can't imagine why you felt shy because she is so nice.

I miss Gran. I wish she hadn't died so I could ask her about Pocket. They sent me here because she went here. Dad said she *loved* it. Maybe he made that up so he and April could get married and not have to deal with me.

When I was in the sitting room downstairs, I sat in the big armchair I always see Miss Sparring in after meals. "Now, Miss Birdie, hem-hem," I said in a Miss Sparring voice, which is low and gruff. "I don't want to see you to-ing and fro-ing in the hallways anymore."

Then I jumped up and sat in the little stiff-backed

chair and said in a high-pitched, trembly Miss Birdie voice, "Yes, Miss Sparring, anything you say, Miss Sparring." Miss Birdie is the housemother who is the little old English lady who was in the air raids in London during World War II, and she trembles.

I don't think anyone in my class likes me anymore. Whitney, Collie, Weasle, Ellie, Fish, and I used to play during recess. We had this game where we pretended we were dinosaurs and attacked each other, but now they say that's too childish. They just want to talk about the dance that's coming up with our brother school. Well, Fish still likes to play. That's because he is a boy. He is the only boy at the Pocket School. When his father died, Mrs. Fisk got a job at the school. They allowed Fish to come here even though it's a girls' school. He will stay here until ninth grade, two more years. Then he'll go to our brother school.

Fish has a dead father, and I have a divorced father. Oh, and Lacey has a dead mother.

I guess that's why Lacey and I are here in a boarding school instead of a regular school. As a matter of fact, in art class today, one of the day students said she thought seventh grade was awfully young to be in boarding school. Most of the boarders begin in ninth grade. Whitney said, "I'm here because Daddy is a diplomat and travels all the time, and also my parents want me to be educated in the United States."

Collie said, "I live in the sticks, and there aren't any good schools there."

Then someone asked, "How about you, Lacey?"

"When my mother died, my father said he needed help taking care of me." She said it very quietly, with her head down. Everyone must have felt bad because they forgot to ask me, which is a good thing. I don't want to talk about it.

I hate art class. Miss Herring says we can do anything we want, so mostly we just talk. Well, I used to like that, but now the others are being mean. They rush to get there and fill up one table so Fish and I won't have a place to sit with them. The thing is, I always liked drawing and painting because of Gran. Maybe tomorrow I'll bring my snapshot of Jip and make a painting of him.

Jip died on the same day that Gran did. Isn't that strange?

Wednesday, January 6

When I prowl up and down the hallway at night, I like to picture the crazy old housemothers lying in their beds, snoring away. Well, maybe, they aren't all snoring.

Let's see—Miss Birdie is probably crying out in her

sleep, dreaming the Germans are still dropping bombs on her. Or she is having a nightmare about me, ha-ha.

And then there's Mrs. Prokopovich. She's the one who says she was married to a Russian count. "Whiskey," she moans. "I want more whiskey." The older girls say she sits in her room and drinks booze when she's off duty.

I bet Miss Perkins, the Latin teacher, is dreaming she is wearing a red dress because in real life she only wears black suits. I wonder why.

Then there is Miss Sparring. What does she do in her sleep? Well, she just plain snores. I can hear her when I stand outside her doorway.

I think I will go prowling again. I will dance down the stairs like a ballet dancer. I will imagine that I have long hair and I am tall and willowy like Lacey, instead of short with short hair. At least I am as strong and muscley as a dancer, and that is from chopping wood for Gran.

Right now I can picture Gran perfectly, the way she would be if she hadn't died. She is sitting by the wood-stove in the house at Hidden Lake. I can picture Mom, too, sitting by her radiator in her little apartment in Minnesota, correcting seventh-grade papers. She would have been my English teacher this year, but no, I am away at boarding school.

Dad-and-April said I had to go away to boarding school. They said I couldn't keep on living in two places and going to two schools, half the year in Minnesota and half the year in Boston. They said I wasn't getting an education, so boarding school it is, the Florence T. Pocket School in Mills, Massachusetts.

I have to admit that going to two schools in the same year was hard. I would start to make friends in Minnesota, but then after Christmas I'd have to leave and go to the school in Boston. The girls in the Boston school never did like me very much. April said it was because every time I came back from Minnesota, I had become so midwestern.

Well, everything was just hunky-dory here at first. Everyone was really nice to me, maybe because I'm little, and they thought I was cute. Whitney, Collie, Lacey, and I were all new seventh-grade boarders together. It was really fun because we were in one room at the end of the hall. I was even almost popular because I would think of the fun things to do. But after a while, Whitney and Collie began to hang out with some of the day students like Weasle and Ellie, and they began to say I was immature. We changed rooms at the end of the term, and now Whitney and Collie are rooming together upstairs. Lacey and I are still together in a smaller room, but Lacey is so quiet.

The teachers were really nice to me, too, in the beginning, because they knew I had been in and out of different schools. Unfortunately lately they've been pestering me. "No more excuses, Lydia," they say. "It's time for you to buckle down."

Whitney said I was only allowed to come because my grandmother went to Pocket. She said otherwise Pocket would never have accepted me because my education has been so bad, and I'm too immature to handle being away at school.

Now it is late enough for me to go prowling again.

Later . . .

I can't believe what happened to me tonight. I'm going to write it all down fast before I forget.

I went into the sitting room near the front door where guests come and sit, and wait to see people. There's another portrait of Miss Pocket in there. It is of just her face when she was young. She looks nice—less prim and proper in this painting. Miss Herring told me yesterday that Miss Pocket was an artist herself. She started Pocket as an art school for girls. I wonder if that's why Gran liked art so much. I think Gran was a pretty good artist, actually. I remember the paintings in her house in New Hampshire, of her view, and of mountains and things. One I have always loved is of a girl sitting with a kitten.

There is also a desk in the front sitting room.

This desk has two drawers with brass handles. You can't look at a desk like that and not want to see what's in it. At least I can't. I pulled the top drawer open and saw a little notebook. On the cover of the little notebook it said Faculty Meeting Notes. You can't look at a book like that and not open it. Guess what? I found out what they talk about at faculty meetings. Uniforms and schedules, and oh yes, Lydia Rice. "Lydia Rice doesn't pay attention in class and talks too much, and she is distracting. Extra study halls for Lydia Rice. Demerits for Lydia Rice because she is not in uniform and her room is messy." I could just hear Miss Sparring saying all this. I felt like writing in the notebook: "The Mad Prowler is watching you. Be careful of what you say." But I won't. Even I am not that dumb.

I decided to strike out for new territory—past the mail cubbies and down the stairs to the ground floor.

On the way down, I stopped for a second and looked at the mural that's painted on the wall at the bottom of the stairs. The paint is cracked and faded in some places, bumpy and grainy in others. I like it a lot. It says POCKET GIRLS on the bottom and shows Pocket girls sitting or playing outside under a tree. One of the girls is jumping rope. It's a tradition at the school, I don't know why, to rub her nose as you walk by and make a wish. Girls have been rubbing her nose for so long, it has pretty much rubbed away.

I came down the rest of the stairs and rubbed the jump-rope girl's nose and made a wish. Or maybe it was a prayer. I always wish (or pray) the same thing: "Please don't let me have to stay here at the Florence T. Pocket School."

Then I kept walking down the hall, past the day students' kitchen and the day students' lunchroom. At the end of the hallway is a door to the outside. It is marked EXIT. I could exit out that door if I wanted to. But up until tonight I have never dared push the door open. I've been scared that it might lock behind me, and I'd be stuck outside. Then I'd really get in trouble. Dad-and-April would find out, and then I don't know what would happen. Besides, the Mad Prowler usually only wears thin socks—all the better to prowl with, my dear, but not good for walking outside.

But tonight I really wanted to go outside and breathe in air that wasn't stale, musty Pocket School air. The air is always too hot and smells like burned dust and old-lady perfume.

I put my hand on the doorknob and pushed. It was a big heavy door, and I had to heave my shoulder against it. The next thing I knew, a hand was on my arm. I looked and saw a man with a white beard. I screamed, and he yelled.

"Blast blistering bleeding crustaceans!" the man

shouted. "You scared me witless. What are you doing? Running away?"

"I wasn't running away," I said. "I just wanted some fresh air. What are you doing here in the middle of the night, anyway?"

The man laughed, and a million deep lines jumped into his face and around his eyes. He smelled of paint and wood shavings, which was actually a comforting kind of smell. "What a thing to ask! I should be asking *you*! I'm the maintenance man by day and the night watchman by night. Name is Howie." He put out a hand.

"Oh, I recognize you now. I've seen you fixing things around school. My name is Lydia Rice," I said, shaking Howie's hand.

"What are you doing up in the middle of the night, Lydia?" he asked.

"I don't know," I said. "I can't sleep, and I hate just sitting in my bed, being wide awake."

"A young lady like you needs her sleep," said Howie.

"Yeah, but I'm not a young lady," I said.

"You look like one to me," said Howie.

"Calling me a young lady makes me sound like I sit still and drink tea or something," I said.

"Well, I guess I can see you don't sit still much. You're kind of a wiry little sprite. A young one, too. What's a young one like you doing away from home?"

"My grandmother made me go," I lied. I didn't want to explain about the divorce and Dad-and-April and living in two places at once. I thought of an easy way to explain things. "I live in Australia, and my grandmother wanted me to be educated in the United States. She went to school here."

"Is that right?" Howie looked thoughtful. I couldn't tell what he was thinking, but he sure was staring at me. Maybe he knew I was lying. "Your grandmother went here, did she? Who might she be?"

"Louisa Rice," I said. "Why? Did you know her?" I was worried that if he did know her, he'd know she wasn't alive anymore.

"Well, I might have," he said. "I have been around this school for a while. Louisa Rice," he repeated. "That would be her married name?"

"Well, yes, I think so."

"You happen to recall the name she had before she married?"

"I don't think so," I said. "I didn't know her before she was married." I knew I was being a smart aleck. "I didn't even know my grandpa. He died before I was born. To tell the truth, before I came to this school, I never even thought about Gran as young or anything. She was just my grandmother."

"That's natural enough," said Howie. "Now let's get

to why you're not tucked fast asleep in bed. Don't they run you around enough? You must be taking some kind of physical education."

The cold air was coming in under the door, and my feet were icy. I was beginning to shiver. "I take dance," I said.

"Well, that should wear you out," he said.

"Naw, it's dumb," I said. "We don't do anything." I didn't explain how I was taking dance because for winter sports all you can do is basketball or dance. I hate basketball, or maybe it's because Whitney, Weasle, and Collie take basketball. Even though I look like I wouldn't like ballet, I do. But dance at Pocket turns out to be modern dance, and it is really goofy. The teacher can't handle us. For the past two classes, I have been hiding behind the curtains in back of the stage. The dumb teacher hasn't even noticed.

Howie's eyes squinched up in the middle of all my thinking about it. "Are you going to report me?" I asked.

He stopped squinching, smiled, and said, "I'm figuring out if you'd like to become a wizard."

"A wizard? What do you mean?"

"What would you like to be if you could be anything? A deer? Or a stone wall? I've often thought it would be restful to be an apple tree. But you, well, perhaps, you'd like to be a penguin, judging from the way you're bobbing around right now."

I was bobbing from foot to foot because my feet were freezing. When he said that, I could imagine I was a penguin, and it made me laugh.

"Shh, now listen, Lydia," he said. "This is what wizards are good for: Say you get an urge to be something different, so you go outside on a night like this. There has to be a moon, you understand, because the moon is what helps the magic. You find a wizard and ask him, or her, to change you into a penguin. He, or she, will chant the spell slowly and quietly."

Howie's voice became slow and quiet here, almost a whisper. "For, you know, when a wizard is chanting spells, his, or her voice is as muted and mysterious as a bell tolling underwater."

I think that's what he said. He talked like a book. He had a funny look in his eyes, too, which made me shiver even more. I couldn't tell if he was joking or serious.

"The next thing you know," he went on, "you will feel yourself shrinking—and bingo—you'll be wearing the black and white suit of a penguin, and off you'll bobble. Wizards, of course, can also turn penguins into people."

Howie walked into the day students' lunchroom, and I followed him. Through the windows I could see the courtyard lit up in the moonlight. It was all dreamy and gleamy with the maple tree we aren't allowed to climb right in the middle. I could see all the Pocket buildings, too, in a square around the courtyard: the classroom buildings and the other big dormitory across from us, and the houses that used to be real houses but are now where girls and old-lady housemothers live.

"You know your Latin teacher, Miss Perkins?" Howie asked. "*She* was a penguin."

I burst out laughing. I was sitting on a lunch table, swinging my legs and laughing my head off. I couldn't remember the last time I had laughed like that. Howie was so right! Miss Perkins, my Latin teacher, was just like a penguin. When she walked she wobbled from side to side; not only that, there were all those black suits! Howie laughed, too. I stared at him with his white hair and white beard. He didn't seem ordinary—he seemed sort of dreamy and gleamy, too.

Now he was staring back at me and pulling on his beard. "You might have the makings to be one," he said. "It's been years and years since I've had an apprentice, but—"

"What do you mean?" I interrupted.

"You could apprentice to be a wizard. We'll find out soon enough what you're made of."

"Find out what I am made of," I repeated. My skin felt jumpy. "No thanks," I said.

Howie raised his eyebrows, which are a bit tangly. "Okay," he said, getting up from the table and walking out of the lunchroom. He walked to the end of the hall-way. "I just thought you—oh well, maybe you ought to be getting back to bed." He stopped in front of the mural. "Well, Lydia, good night now. Off you go." There was a door right there, and he opened it and disappeared behind it.

I felt cold and lonely.

On the door I noticed a tiny little sign with a funny little wizard, wearing a pointy hat covered with stars painted on it. SILLY WIZARD WITHIN said the sign.

I knocked on the door, and Howie's head appeared. "What's a Silly Wizard?" I asked.

"A wizard who doesn't take himself too seriously," he said.

"Is that the kind of wizard I could be?" I asked.

"Oh yes, of course. I forgot to tell you that, didn't I?"

"Maybe I would like to be your apprentice," I said.

"Think about it and find me in this hallway at 4:35," he said and shut the door.

So here I am, thinking about it. Is he just a crazy old man? He doesn't seem crazy. He seems cozy. Like Santa Claus.

Thursday, January 7

Tonight I have a lot to write about. I hope I can get it all down. So here goes.

At 4:35, after dance (well, after hiding out from dance), I went to Howie's door. I knocked on it.

He halfway came out and said, "Oh, it's you. What are you doing here?"

He seemed so surprised to see me that for a minute I thought maybe I had dreamed everything.

"You said I could become a wizard," I said.

"You sure that's what you want?" he asked.

A stream of sweaty girls in shorts and sneakers walked by. It was really noisy for a moment, all their feet pounding up the stairs. Collie and Whitney were in the pack, laughing their heads off. I don't think anyone even noticed Howie and me, standing in the corner on the other side of the stairs.

"No, I really want to know," I said. "I just hate it when people *want* me to do things. It makes me not want to do them."

Howie came all the way out of his door and stood next to the mural. He smiled and said, "I know what you mean."

A lot of people say that. I know what you mean. But Howie, when he said it, I believed him.

"So tell me what I have to do," I said.

"You have tasks."

"What sort of tasks?" I asked.

"To start with, a wizard should know a certain number of little interesting facts unknown to most people, facts that make you aware of your universe, the world you live in. You happen to be living in the Pocket world."

"So what do I have to do?"

He stroked his beard. "We'll start right here with this painting." He pointed to the mural. "Tell me what you see, beginning with the border."

"Okay," I said. "The border goes all the way around the picture. It says POCKET GIRLS on the bottom. On the left side are the letters of the alphabet, A–B–C–D–E. They are painted in white paint, I guess, but it's sort of yellow in places."

"Old paint yellows," he said. "And on the right, what do you see?"

"It spells WHEEL," I said. "Why? What does it mean?"

"Aha," he said. "Curiosity is an important attribute for an apprentice. Go on."

"Well, at the bottom, in the right-hand corner," I said pointing, "there's a P. P for Pocket, I suppose. Gee, I bet Miss Pocket painted it." I felt proud of myself. Howie was smiling, so I guessed I was on the right track.

"Well, this was in the old days because the girls are wearing bloomers and old-fashioned-looking sailor-suit tops. The jump-rope girl has really long braids, and she doesn't have a nose because it's been rubbed off."

I pointed to each girl as I talked about her.

"That girl is standing in front of an easel. She's painting a picture. Another girl is sitting on the grass, reading a book. This one is sitting with a white kitten in her lap. And *this* girl is up in the tree, and she has a big grin on her face. I'd be grinning, too, if I could be in that tree."

Then I looked at the tree again. "That's the same tree that's in the courtyard," I said, "because some of the same houses are in the background. They must have turned the grass those girls are sitting on into the courtyard. And how come they don't let us climb the tree?"

"Not ladylike," Howie said, his eyes twinkling. He *is* like Santa Claus. "Now here's your task, Lydia." He pointed to the mural. His finger was thick and stubby. "Find out who these girls are."

"They were *real?*" I asked.

"Of course," he said.

"When? How long ago?"

"I knew you'd make a good apprentice," he said. He smiled at me again. I felt my heart squeeze. I couldn't remember the last time someone had smiled at me because they were pleased with me. "Your task is to find out who these girls were, and while you're at it, see if you can figure out why these letters are in the border. Now it's time for my dinner and time for you to go up and change for dinner."

"Already? I have to go now?"

"I have to eat sometime," he said.

"Where do you eat?" I asked.

He pointed to the day-students' kitchen. "I eat in

there with Nellie, the cook, and the rest of the kitchen staff. They grab a bite before it's time to feed you lot."

"Oh," I said. It was the first time I even thought about the Pocket cook and the maids eating their own dinner.

"So, off you go. *Rach manji.*"

"What?"

"*Rach manji.* That is what wizards say when they are parting. You answer back, *Naji, naji.*"

"*Naji, naji,*" I said, laughing a little, and then I went leaping up the stairs because I was happy for once. I went to my room and changed for dinner.

Now it is night and I am writing by flashlight and thinking about Howie.

I can just hear April. "You are too old to be playing at wizards, and we are not sending you to an expensive girls' school so you can spend time socializing with the maintenance man."

I have been waving my flashlight around the room and can see which side of the room is neat and which is messy. Start with Lacey's side. On her bureau is a picture of her mother, father, and Lacey when she was little. She is wearing a pretty lacy (of course) dress. The background of the photograph is misty, and her parents' heads are touching. I guess her parents loved each other. It must be horrible to have a dead mother. Maybe that's why it seems as if she is put together with Scotch tape.

She takes dance, too, and hides in the corners hoping not be noticed. She reminds me of a moth caught in a cobweb. If we were friends, I would ask her to hide behind the stage curtains with me, but I know I can't ask her to do bad things.

Next to the picture of her parents, all lined up, casting little shadows, are her perfume, lipstick, a box of jewelry, hairbrush, comb. Next is her desk. Her books are in her book bag (not scattered all over the place like mine), and the book bag is on the floor next to the chair, sitting ready to go to school tomorrow. Her blazer is hanging on the back of her chair. It is not wrinkled.

I have to wade through clothes, books, book bag, and my water clock to get to my bed. Over vacation I saw a really neat clock in a junk store near our apartment in Minneapolis. There were some pretty great things in there, but this clock was the best. The way it works is that water drips slowly from one container to the next, and the containers are attached to a cog at the back of the face of the clock. As the containers get heavier, the hands turn. In the end, the water gets sucked back up to the top and starts dripping all over again.

As soon as I saw it, I knew I wanted to try to make one like it; then it was time to go to Boston. I can't do stuff like that in Boston. I can't make messes in April's house.

When I got back here, though, I started to make one. I know there are some things I can't figure out, like how to make the water go back up to the top, but I can try to get the hands to move. I ripped off the back of my Pocket tablet of theme paper to make the face of the clock, and I am using empty frozen orange juice cans for the water containers. I asked Nellie to save them for me. After school today I poked a hole in the bottom of the cans, but I think the holes are too big. The water comes out too fast. My bed got soaked, and I had to pull the blankets off.

Now I am pulling the blankets back up on my bed and turning them so the damp part is at my feet.

How do I find out who the girls in the painting are? Tomorrow I will begin. Tomorrow Lacey will say in her soft southern accent, "Get up, Lydia." I will open my eyes, and my first thought will be that I haven't done my homework again.

Tomorrow Miss Birdie will stick her head in the doorway and say, "Late, late, late," clicking her tongue against her false teeth.

And I will say, "Late, late, late," mocking her English accent.

And she will say, "Lydia Rice, I shall report you to Miss Sparring," and hold up a trembly hand and wag a finger at me.

And I will wag a finger back at her and say, "Go

ahead." I am not afraid of Miss Birdie. I know she won't report me because she is more afraid of Miss Sparring than I am.

Friday, January 8

Here is what I did today.

First, I got dressed in my stupid uniform. My skirt is too long for me so I have taken a stapler and shortened it. The staples are coming out, and they scratch my legs. My uniform blazer is too big, but there's nothing I can do about that. The only uniform blouse I could find has a stain down the front of it where I spilled baked beans a few days ago.

I went downstairs, taking my time because I could smell the sausages from the dining room and I hate Pocket sausages. They are shriveled and greasy, and make me think of chopped-off dead fingers. If there are sausages, that means waffles. I hate Pocket waffles. They are like cardboard, and the maple syrup is watery and doesn't taste like anything. Real maple syrup is thick. When you eat it you can taste spring coming. I know because sometimes we visited Gran in New Hampshire in March and made the real stuff. I remember it was when the sun was warm in the day, and the snow had melted until it was in patches. There were little snow fleas hopping about, and the smell of the ground came up. You could see the stone walls coming out from being buried; they looked like dinosaur bones.

Anyway Mrs. Fisk is the housemother who is the head of my new table. It means that for the next few weeks, I have to sit with Fish. This morning when I sat down, everyone was already in the dining room, and they had started eating. Fish said, "You're late, Lydia."

"Oh, really?" I said.

Fish, which is what everyone calls him even though his name is Alexander, has goggly eyes like a fish; his last name is Fisk, which sounds like fish. He has too many teeth, and they are too big for his mouth. He lives with his mother in Corner House where she is a house-mother.

Fish is a pest. Everyone is pretty mean to him, but he doesn't seem to notice. His mother doesn't seem to notice, either. She is kind of vague, as if Fish doesn't really belong to her. Usually it is very quiet at breakfast because everyone is still waking up, but with Fish at the table, it is like diving into a cold lake. He is very loud and starts off the day with stupid announcements. Today he said, "Yesterday I found a hair in the ravioli. It was a gray hair. Do you think it was Nellie's?"

No one said anything.

"A cockroach can live eight days without a head," he

said. Everyone kept ignoring him, but Fish doesn't really get when to stop, and he eats with his mouth open. This morning I could see waffles being ground to a pulp by his big teeth, plus he had fake maple syrup stuck to his face. I didn't want to look at him.

"When I die, I'm going to be on a stamp," he said. "I'm going to have an airport named after me." Whitney, who is at our table, was looking at him as if she wanted to kill him. He stared straight at her and said, "You are going to have a toilet named after you."

A hand came down on Fish's shoulder. It belonged to Mr. O'Hare. "Enough, Fish," he said. He had walked over from the head table. He runs the dining room for breakfast, probably so Mr. Wing can lounge in bed. "We can hear you all over the dining room. Can you not hear the hushed stillness of a room full of people who are not ready yet to be awake, a room full of people still in their dreams?" (This is the way Mr. O'Hare always talks.) "Your high-pitched voice, Fish, is just too much to take, so use your mouth to put food into, good, nourishing food. Chew carefully, with your mouth shut, please, and keep your utterances unto yourself."

Mr. O'Hare lives in an apartment in the same house with Mrs. Fisk. I guess Mrs. Fisk is used to Mr. O'Hare talking like this to her son. She just smiled, looked vague, and said, "Thank you, Vernon, you are absolutely right. Alexander, please do keep your voice down. Anyone who is finished may be excused. Lydia, you and Alexander may see that the table gets cleared. I have to rush off this morning. Oh, and Alexander, I want you to come over to my office right after school gets out today because you have a doctor's appointment."

I couldn't help myself. My curiosity got the better of me. I found myself actually looking at Fish, which can be difficult because not only does he have goggly eyes, he also has these goofy dimples like big gashes around the corners of his mouth. I asked, "Just what does your mother do besides being a housemother?"

"She tutors kids and she tests them, their IQs, you know, stuff like that."

"IQs?"

"IQ. Intelligence quotient. How smart you are."

"How smart you are?"

"Yeah. Hasn't she given you the test yet? She gives one to all the new students." He looked me over with his ugly eyes. "But maybe she's avoiding you because she's afraid of what she'll find. Or won't find."

"Ha-ha." I stretched out a leg and gave him a good hard kick.

"Just kidding," he said. "She'll get to you soon enough."

"What if I flunk it?"

"You can't flunk an intelligence test; it's not like that. And besides, it's easy. She asks you proverbs and what they mean, and you have to remember lists of numbers and say them backward."

"*Backward?* Why?"

"Because it's a sign of intelligence to remember stuff backward. She takes all your answers and comes up with a number, and that's how smart you are."

I played with waffle crumbs on the table and tried to think about all that. Mrs. Fisk giving intelligence tests! She seemed too vague to do something like that. What if she got it wrong and put down the wrong number? Fish got up and started stacking plates onto a tray. As he cleared the glasses, I wondered if people were like glasses, with a certain amount of intelligence in them. Very full. Half empty.

I have never thought about smartness in that way before. Somehow I don't feel like a glass. I am more like an electric appliance. Sometimes I am plugged in, and sometimes I am not.

Anyway maybe Mrs. Fisk has forgotten to test me, and now that I am sitting at her table, she'll remember. The last thing I need in my life is to find out exactly how dumb I am. So I have decided I can't sit at her table anymore.

At recess I saw Howie across the courtyard. He was fixing a door handle. I was going to go over and say hi, but then I remembered my task. I thought I ought to get going on it. I tore some paper off of my theme tablet and stood in the hallway in front of the mural and sketched it so I would remember it better. The bell for the end of recess rang, but I kept drawing. Mr. O'Hare passed me. He said, "Lydia Rice, what are you doing? You are going to be late to history class."

"Mr. O'Hare, do you know who the girls in this mural are?" I asked.

He studied the painting for a moment and said, "Charity, Hope, Prudence, Constance, Faith."

"Really?" I asked, excited.

Mr. O'Hare smirked. "No, not really, but they seem like appropriate names for those girls."

"Oh," I said. "Well, what do you think these letters mean?" I pointed to ABCDE and WHEEL.

"A–B–C–D–E. It's the alphabet. The basic tool for learning. And WHEEL, I have always supposed, has to do with the wheel of life, the turning of time."

I shook my head. It sounded like baloney to me. Why couldn't he just say, "I don't know; I have no idea," instead of having to have an answer. "Now come along, Lydia, let's not be dawdling."

"But you're a history teacher," I said, "and this is a history question. When did kids wear clothes like that?"

Ha! I had him. He put on a I-am-a-serious-history-teacher look.

"At the turn of the century," he said. "Perhaps all the way up to the 1920s, '30s."

"Is there anything at all you see that might give you an exact date?"

Mr. O'Hare studied the mural some more and finally pointed to the P in the corner. "P . . . Miss Pocket," he said. "She ran the school from 1890 to 1920, so sometime in there."

Then he dragged me off to class. It was not a good class. He started by complaining about the tests we had taken yesterday. He complains about us all the time. He says girls are not interested in history; they are only interested in the present, and in the present they are only interested in hair and in letters from boys. I'm not like that at all, and he complains about me the most.

At the beginning of the year, Fish told me Mr. O'Hare has a pig heart in his closet. "A pig heart?" I asked. "What do you mean, a pig heart?"

"The heart of a pig," he said.

"Why?" I asked.

"Someone gave it to him as a present, and he keeps it in there."

"Why would someone give Mr. O'Hare the heart of a pig? And why would he keep it in his closet? Wouldn't it smell?"

"He keeps it in formaldehyde."

"That is the strangest thing I have ever heard," I said.

Fish is full of very strange information. I can't help thinking about that pig heart every time I am in Mr. O'Hare's class. I picture it beating away there by itself. It is hard to concentrate on the French Revolution.

Saturday, January 9

One of these nights the Mad Prowler will prowl across the courtyard, go into Mr. O'Hare's classroom, open his closet, and look inside. But Fish says the closet is always locked. Besides, I would be very afraid. Imagine looking at a pig heart in the middle of the night.

At supper I tried sitting at Miss Birdie's table instead of Mrs. Fisk's because I didn't want Mrs. Fisk to remember she was supposed to give me an IQ test. I thought Miss Birdie might not realize I wasn't supposed to sit at her table because she never really knows what kids are supposed to be doing. But Miss Sparring happened to be walking by just as I was sitting down. She said, "Hem-hem, what are you doing here, Lydia? You are supposed to be with Mrs. Fisk. I made up the table list myself." I had to go and sit right next to Mrs. Fisk because I was the last one at the table, and no one ever wants to sit right next to the housemother.

"Stop chewing with your mouth open," Whitney was saying to Fish.

"I'm not," said Fish with his mouth full of food.

"Stop looking at me," said Whitney.

"Who would want to look at you?"

"Do we really have to sit with these babies?" Terry Bates, who is a junior, asked.

"I think it's nice to have young kids around," said Lisa Smalley, who is another junior. "It feels more like home."

"Not any home I would like to be in," said Terry.

"Don't you ever cut your nails?" Whitney asked Fish. "They're disgusting."

Everyone looked at Fish's hands. His fingernails were long and dirty.

"So?" he said. "They're good for picking at things with."

Everyone groaned. Mrs. Fisk said, "That's enough, Alexander."

We had apples for dessert. Starting at the top of her apple, Mrs. Fisk went around and around it with her knife. She pared off the whole peel without it breaking. "If you can do that," she said, "you will have good luck." So we all tried, and guess what! I was the only one who did it without the peel breaking.

I can't sleep even though it's almost midnight. I think I'll go prowling, but I'll have to wait a little longer. Everyone stays up later on Saturday night.

Later . . .

Guess what, guess what, guess what! I did go prowling and I thought I'd see what the latest scoop was in the faculty meeting notes. I was a little nervous about running into Howie because I knew he wouldn't like it if he saw me wandering around at night again, but I was also pretty sure he wouldn't come upstairs to this floor.

I was about to open the drawer to the desk where the faculty meeting notes are kept, when a book on top of the desk caught my eye. It was a book for kids, with a picture of two girls jumping rope. I picked it up. It looked pretty old and used. The cloth part of the cover was worn in places, and there were nicks in the gold border around the picture. But get this: One of the girls had long braids, just like the jump-rope girl in the mural. It was called *Best Friends* and was written and illustrated by Elizabeth Longford. I opened the book, and there was this spidery old-fashioned writing on the inside first page where they put the title. It said, "To all the Pocket girls, with warm wishes, Elizabeth Longford."

I sat right down in the biggest armchair and read the book. It wasn't very long. It was about two girls, Jane and Maisie, who lived near each other and were best friends. They did everything together and made up jump-rope rhymes together. They had this clothesline hooked up between their two bedroom windows so they could send messages back and forth. They wrote the messages in a code only they could understand. Whenever they needed extra luck, they rubbed their noses, because once Jane was rubbing her nose when she found two dimes on the sidewalk so they were able to get ice cream when the Good Humor man came. But then a new girl, Harriet, moved next to them, and the girls started fighting because Harriet made them jealous of each other. She made them feel that rubbing their noses, the jump-rope rhymes, and the codes they made up were silly.

I know just the sort of girl Harriet is. She is just like Weasle, pretending to be your friend and then saying mean things about you behind your back. But Jane and Maisie finally figured it out, and they stopped playing with her. Harriet was sad and lonely then, and I like how Elizabeth Longford wrote it because actually you do feel kind of sorry for Harriet, even though she deserved what she got. But then Jane figured out jumping rope would be more fun if they had three people because two people could swing one big rope and the other person could jump. They asked Harriet to play, and Harriet was so happy to be asked that she got a lot nicer. By the end all three girls were making up rhymes and rubbing their noses, and Harriet had a message clothesline going to her house, too.

It is a good story, and the pictures are great with lots of detail. I like the way the girls look. They have messy hair, scrapes on their knees, and things like that.

The Jane in the story looks like the jump-rope girl in the mural. I wonder if Elizabeth Longford was the jump-rope girl. The book was published by Wagner Brothers in New York in 1952. Maybe I can write to Wagner Brothers, and they will know where Elizabeth Longford is.

Should I tell Howie what I suspect, or should I wait?

Dear Elizabeth Longford,

I just found your book *Best Friends*. I like it a lot, and I really like the drawings. I go to the Pocket School, and I think you must be one of the girls in the mural that is at the bottom of the stairs in Pocket House. Am I right? Every time we go by the jump-rope girl, we rub her nose for good luck. Her nose has been worn away.

Would you mind writing and telling me if you are in the mural, which girl you are, and who the other girls in the mural are? Can you tell me as much about it as you know? For instance, what ABCDE WHEEL means in the border?

Can you tell me if you were homesick at all when you went to Pocket? Did you know being able to pare off the peel of a whole apple without it breaking is also good luck?

Sincerely,
Lydia Rice

Sunday, January 10

Sunday is the most boring day in the world.

Monday, January 11

At 4:35 today I went and knocked on Howie's door. He came right out and said, "I have been expecting you."

I said, "You have?"

He said, "Not really, but I am glad to see you."

The door to his room was wide open. Being the nosy type I looked in. I saw a big board with rows and rows of keys hanging on hooks. Underneath each hook was a label like POCKET HALL or DUCKWORTH #1 or DUCK-WORTH #2.

"Are those the keys to the whole school?" I wanted to know.

He said, "Pretty much, yes."

"Do you have closet keys?" I asked, thinking of Mr. O'Hare's closet and the pig heart.

"Closet keys?" he asked.

"If you wanted to get into a closet, say in Mr. O'Hare's classroom?"

"The room keys open the closets," he said. "Why would you want to know something like that?"

"Fish, who is the only boy here—"

"I know who he is," said Howie. "It can't be easy being the only boy at Pocket. But on the other hand, a kid like that'd probably get eaten alive at a boys' school, so it's probably a good thing he is here."

"Well, Fish told me Mr. O'Hare has a pig heart in his closet, but it's always locked so there's no way of knowing."

"A pig heart," said Howie. "That's very interesting. Do you think it's still beating? The telltale pig heart," he said with a laugh.

"That's exactly how I picture it," I said. "Just sitting there in his closet, beating away. It gives me the creeps."

Howie laughed again. Then I pushed past him a bit so I could see the rest of the room.

Some of the room is for maintenance and stuff. There are tools hanging on the wall and a workbench and a chest of cute little drawers that say things like NAILS and SCREWS. There is a shelf with very big flashlights and a list posted with important telephone numbers for Fire, Police, electrician, plumber, and also for insect exterminators.

In one corner there's a sort of a cot with blankets on it. I guess Howie must take naps there, between being a maintenance man and a night watchman.

There are watercolor paintings all over the walls! There are a couple that are of wizards with long beards and tall pointed caps. There is one of a boy who is also a tree so his arms are branches and his feet are roots. My favorite is one of a spider playing a harp with two of its hairy legs. It is a funny picture, I think. Who would ever think of a spider playing a harp?

"Wow, Howie, did you paint these?" I asked.

He nodded.

"They're Silly Wizard things?"

Howie nodded again.

"I love them," I said. "You are really a good artist."

"Thank you," he said.

"You should be the art teacher."

He looked interested. "Why is that?" he asked.

"Miss Herring is terrible. We don't *do* anything."

Now he looked troubled. "I guess I knew that. I've been by the art room." He pulled on his beard. "It is a shame," he said. "Pocket used to be a place where girls learned to paint and draw."

"Why don't you say something to Mr. Wing about it?" I asked.

Howie put back his head and laughed. "Me? Me say something to Mr. Wing?"

"Well, you've been around a long time. You should tell him how it used to be."

He shook his head. "How are you doing with your task?"

"I might actually be on to something."

"Really?" Howie looked excited.

"But I don't want to tell you yet cuz I don't know for sure." I had been going to tell him about Elizabeth Longford's book, and then I decided I'd wait until I knew more.

"You'll figure it out. I know you will."

That's why I like Howie. He believes in me.

I noticed behind Howie was a desk with a photograph on it. It was of a pretty woman with long dark hair and big dark eyes. "Who is that?" I asked.

"My wife," he said. He kind of barked it out and turned away.

The way he said it made me not want to ask any more questions. And then anyhow he said it was time for him to eat supper. "*Rach manji,*" he said.

"*Naji, naji,*" I said.

Tuesday, January 12

Today my conscience got the better of me. I decided not to hide during dance class; besides, it's boring skipping it, maybe even more boring than going to the class. The creepy thing is the dance teacher doesn't notice me when I *am* there and doesn't notice me when I'm *not* there. She never takes attendance or anything. The trouble is, I have no idea what's going on anymore, and now it's hard, not just dumb. There are girls in the class who think they are Isadora Duncan. They act cold and snotty toward me because I bumble around. Personally I think the class is kind of funny, but some people have no sense of humor.

After dance I really wanted to see a human being I could talk to because I was feeling crummy, and I was hoping I could find Howie.

I found him sitting in the day student's lunchroom, eating his supper at one of the long tables.

"Got to eat early tonight," he said. "Thought I might try to catch you on your way back from sports."

"That looks good," I said, looking at his plate. "Did Nellie make that?" He nodded as I pulled out a bench and sat down opposite him.

"I have noticed," he said, smiling, "that she makes better meals for the staff than she does for you."

"Huh," I said. "That figures." I put my arms on the table and rested my head on them. I was feeling tired and hungry, and sick of the Pocket School.

"Not a great day, huh?" he asked.

"No," I said.

"Winter is a tough time in a boarding school."

"Anytime is a tough time in a boarding school."

Howie put down his fork and held up a big envelope. It was one of those envelopes they call vanilla or manila or something like that. Important things usually come in them. "The reason I wanted to catch you is that I have something for you. It might cheer you up and it will also teach you some things about being a Silly Wizard."

He handed the envelope to me. "Read it after you've finished your homework," he said.

But of course I didn't wait until I'd done my homework. After saying *rach manji* to him, I went upstairs and started reading the story that was in the envelope. I finished it in study hall.

Now I know why Howie sounded like a book that night he was telling me about people being turned into penguins. It's because he has written it all down as a story.

Miss Howl, Once an Owl

As everyone knows, the moon is magic, but it takes a Silly Wizard to perform the magic.

If, for instance, you'd like to be a penguin for a while, you find a Silly Wizard. You go outside on a moonlit night and ask him, or her, to change you into a penguin. He, or she, will chant the spell slowly and quietly, for when a wizard (even a silly one) is chanting spells, his or her voice is as muted and as mysterious as a bell tolling underwater.

The next thing you know, you feel yourself shrinking. In the next breath you take, you're wearing the black-and-white suit of a penguin, and off you bobble.

Penguins, of course, can also become people; a bear can become a man; a fern may be a boy; a girl, a pelican. An old woman may even choose to become a blade of grass . . .

. . . and that is what Silly Wizards are good for.

In this story it so happens that an owl wanted to be a girl.

This particular owl spent every night of her life swooping above the moonlit black-and-white world. Hunger drove her, and the thrill of the kill. She would spy a mouse cowering in the tall grass and dive with terrifying speed. There would be the satisfying crunch of bones. All night she would hunt until it was time to rest.

Such was the owl's life: hunting by night, sleeping by day. But one dusk on her way to work, she happened to fly over a courtyard of a school; and she was caught momentarily by the sound of laughter. It was a group of girls who were outside playing tag.

The owl perched on the branch of a maple tree that grew in the middle of the courtyard. For a long time she watched the girls running, laughing, and playing. If only I could run and laugh and play, too, she thought. I will find a Silly Wizard and ask to be turned into a girl.

Now it just so happened that a Silly Wizard was working at the school. His name was Mr. Old. He was the maintenance man by day and the night watchman by night.

That evening after the girls had gone away, he happened to be making his rounds when the owl spotted him. Ordinarily you don't know a Silly Wizard, but the owl looked down on Mr. Old and knew him immediately for what he was.

Just as Mr. Old passed the tree, the owl called, "Silly Wizard!"

"Hello, Owl," Mr. Old replied politely. "What can I do for you?"

"I want to become a girl," said the owl.

Mr. Old looked up at the sky. The moon was waning; it was as weak as a whisper. "Maybe you should wait until the moon is full," he said. "I am afraid the magic might not be strong enough."

"I don't want to wait," the owl said haughtily. "I want to be a girl and play."

"All right," said Mr. Old. "Have it your way. Just remember, I am a Silly Wizard, and things may not come out exactly the way you want, what with the moon being the way it is and everything."

"Get on with it, please," commanded the owl. Her yellow eyes were fierce and unblinking.

Mr. Old leaned against the tree and tried to remember the charm for turning an owl into a girl. At last he spoke:

"Sparkling eyes from the South,
Naughtiness from the North,
Eagerness from the East,
Whistling from the West."

"Are these all the things I will have as a girl?" the owl asked, beginning to feel excited.

"Yes," said Mr. Old. "Now you must hoot seven times." He closed his eyes and listened. On the seventh hoot, he opened his eyes. The owl was gone, and the girl, well, he didn't know where the girl, if she was a girl, had ended up, but he hoped for the best. He let out his breath and continued on his rounds.

The next day, the head of the school, Mrs. Morning, was sitting at her desk, despairing about the seventh grade. The day before, the third seventh-grade teacher she'd hired that year had walked into her office and quit.

All year long someone was causing trouble. Someone was taking notebooks and stuffing them into the trash; someone was starting rumors that ruined the reputations of several girls; someone was scribbling Marie's name all over the walls; someone was going through the lockers and taking things. And no one knew who that someone was.

Mrs. Morning suspected Silas Smooth.

She sighed out of frustration and weariness. No one, not even Mrs. Morning, could catch Silas Smooth. He was better dressed than all the rest. His shoes were shined; his trousers were pressed; his shirts were tucked in; his hair was combed. He carried his homework in a briefcase, and he always got straight A's. His perfect manners charmed the world, and no one could ever actually catch him doing anything wrong.

And yet she thought that it was Silas who was laughing up his sleeve.

This time she'd hire someone special, someone who could really handle kids, a teacher who could read the hearts and minds of seventh graders. Maybe she should teach seventh grade herself. But no, she knew she couldn't teach and also run the school.

Mrs. Morning pushed back her hair, took off her glasses, and rubbed her eyes.

When she put her glasses back on, she saw before her a woman with short white hair, a bony face, and a nose as sharp as a beak. Her mouth didn't seem to want to smile. Mrs. Morning blinked, but the woman stared back without blinking at all. Mrs. Morning shivered without knowing why.

"I've come for the job," said the woman.

"What job?" Mrs. Morning asked.

"I intend to teach the seventh grade, of course," said the woman. She raised one eyebrow. "I believe there is an opening."

"What is your name?" asked Mrs. Morning.

"Miss Howl," said the woman.

"Miss Howl," repeated Mrs. Morning.

What Mrs. Morning wanted to say was, "I wouldn't hire you if you were the last person on earth." But instead she found herself gazing into the unblinking eyes of the woman. Good grief, she thought, she has yellow eyes. I have never seen anyone with yellow eyes before.

Mrs. Morning found herself saying, "You are just the sort of teacher I have been looking for. The seventh grade has been a bit difficult this year and—"

"Can't let them get away with things," Miss Howl interrupted.

"Yes, er, I'll show you to your classroom," said Mrs. Morning.

As it happened Miss Howl was a fright of a

teacher. She was like a scream in the dark. She made those seventh graders sit up and shake. She called Lester, who had pimples, Spots. She called Jessica, who was plump, Tubs. To Martin, who was small for his age, she'd say, "Hey, Pip-Squeak, come up to the board and do the problem, if you can *reach* it." Then she'd hoot with laughter.

Mrs. Morning saw it all and for some reason felt powerless to do anything about it.

And Mr. Old, who also saw it all, figured his spell had gone a bit silly. Miss Howl wasn't a girl at all. She was a witch of a woman who couldn't remember what she'd been, or even why she had wanted to be human. He pulled on his beard and wondered how he could fix things. He couldn't turn Miss Howl back into an owl because there are rules, and one of the rules is a creature must *ask* to be transformed.

But then it occurred to him that maybe he could get someone, some creature, some—some *tree*—yes, that was it—the maple tree in the courtyard—to help her remember that she had been an owl who wanted to be a girl. The maple tree had been wanting to be a boy for a long time.

He pulled on his beard and looked forward to his nightly rounds.

Wednesday, January 13

It was *so* cold today. It was so cold that when I stepped outside to go to assembly, my hair froze into little ice crystals right on my head. My hair was wet because I had just washed it during morning cleanup. Whitney saw me and said, "Anyone with brains should know enough to dry their hair before they go outside." I, myself, think it is actually pretty neat to have icicles all over my head.

I skipped dance class because I couldn't stand the snotty Isadora Duncans flicking back their long hair and prancing around on their long slender legs.

I stopped to see Howie and tell him I *loved* the story and are there more and does the tree turn into a human and is he Mr. Old in the story? He smiled but said he couldn't stay and talk because the pipes had burst in Corner House. He had to do something about it.

Thursday, January 14

I am in study hall. I had a crummy day. I flunked my math test. I got sent out of English class. English class, for crying out loud. I used to love English. This stupid Miss Cherry. All she ever does is make us diagram sentences. I was drawing little people sliding down the little slanty lines we have to draw, and she sent me out. I have to go for a detention study hall on Saturday morning. When everyone came out of English and saw me standing in the hall, Whitney said, "Don't you ever wish you could just be normal?"

Blast blistering bleeding crustaceans!

I am going to write about Christmas in New Hampshire two years ago when we still spent Christmas with Gran.

Gran, Jip, and I went out across frozen Hidden Lake to look for our Christmas tree. We wanted to go across the lake because it seemed as if more evergreens grew on the other side. Gran pulled the sled, and I carried the hatchet. Jip raced along beside us. I wore a red scarf on my head, and Gran said I reminded her of Gretel in the old book of fairy tales she has.

It was snowing very big snowflakes. I remember feeling as if Gran, Jip, and I were on a Christmas card. We reached the other shore. It was dark and mysterious because of all the trees, but when we actually got there, we could see they were crowding so thickly together that they were skinny and not very straight. Mostly they had a lot of branches on one side but not the other. We pulled the sled up the hill, which wasn't easy because of all the poky branches and, where there weren't trees, there were boulders.

We came to a flat place where there was a grove of fat evergreens covered with snow. It looked like a place you could live in or make forts or play hide-and-seek. You could burrow right in under the snowy branches. That's just what Jip did.

We found a perfect tree. Its branches grew evenly all the way around. I cleared the snow away from the bottom of the trunk, took the sheath off the hatchet, and began to chop. The wood inside the cut was wet and green and sticky. I suddenly felt sorry to be chopping the tree down. Gran must have felt the same way.

"We don't have to have a Christmas tree," she said.

"We could lop off some of the branches from those funny trees farther down and decorate the house like that."

"But we always have a Christmas tree," I said. I didn't want anything to be different from the way we had always done things.

"Okay," she said.

I swung the hatchet and chipped away. We should have brought the saw because it would have been a straighter, easier cut, but a hatchet seemed more old-fashioned.

"Tim-ber!" I shouted.

Gran caught the tree and shook off the snow. We tied it to the sled and managed not to lose it on the bumpy ride back down the hill. Together we pulled it home across the ice, each with a hand holding the loop of rope.

"Mush," said Gran, and I barked. Jip stopped running and looked at me with his ears straight up, which made us laugh.

The snow was coming down hard now, not in big flakes, but in small ones. There were so many of them that there weren't any spaces between them. The sky, the lake, and the air were all the same color. Everything was silent and secret. I could feel the silence inside my ears.

It's never quiet at boarding school except in the middle of the night.

When we got the tree into the house, it seemed much bigger than it was when it was outside. We had to saw a couple of inches off the bottom because it didn't quite fit in the living room; even then the top bent a little. We decided we liked how it looked, especially because the bent part made feathery shadows across the ceiling.

Mom made hot chocolate and put on a record of Bing Crosby singing Christmas carols, and Dad and I got out our box of ornaments.

We always made our own ornaments at Hidden Lake. They were made out of all different kinds of things— sometimes from clay, sometimes from cardboard, or from flour and salt that we baked and then painted.

Mom brought me a mug of hot chocolate with marshmallows melting in it. I put the first ornament on, a zebra I had made when I was six, which I had painted in different colored stripes. I wasn't sad about the tree being cut down anymore. I thought it was happy to be our Christmas tree.

Friday, January 15

Today Miss Sparring told me I couldn't work on the water clock in my room anymore. She said I was making too much of a mess. She said, "Hem-hem, you are being selfish and inconsiderate of Lacey. Hem-hem, you are much too old to be tinkering around with trash." She made my face burn. She made worms squirm inside my stomach. I took all the parts of my water clock and threw them away.

Now as I am writing this, I feel like I am Gretel. I have been left out in the woods. I don't know how to get home. I don't even have a Hansel to help me.

Now I am crying and that is dumb.

I am mad at Gran for going to Pocket. If she hadn't come here, I wouldn't be here.

Later...

I put on my jeans, a warm sweater, and thick socks in order to go prowling.

I love being the only one up at night. Ha-ha to Miss Sparring. May she rot in her old-lady nightgown.

Howie was just about to go on his rounds when I came down the stairs. He shook his head when he saw me. "Bad, Lydia," he said. "This is bad. Go back to bed."

"I got sent out of English class today," I said.

He said, "You sound a little bit like Laura."

"Who is Laura?"

"Laura was a girl who got sent out of class by Miss Howl."

"Oh good, more Silly Wizard stuff."

"If you go back upstairs, I'll give you another chapter," he said.

"It's a deal," I said.

He went into his room and came back out with another vanilla-manila envelope.

"*Rach manji*," I said, already racing up the stairs.

"*Naji, naji*," he called after me.

Michael, Once a Maple

Laura was in the seventh grade. She hated Miss Howl, but then she didn't like anything about school. In the fall she had been new. The other girls, who had known each other since they were babies, wouldn't make friends with her. The boys whispered and laughed behind her back. She knew it was partly because she made a point of doing what she wanted to do, such as wearing her favorite green sweater every single day.

Her desk was next to the window. She had a fine view of the maple tree that grew in the middle of the courtyard. "The only nice thing about this school is you," Laura would say, nodding to the tree. She didn't say it out loud, of course, or the kids would have thought she was really strange.

More and more Laura felt drawn to the tree. When Miss Howl scolded her for not paying attention (which happened quite a lot), she pretended that when the tree waved its branches, it was talking to her, telling her not to mind.

Its bare black limbs carved black lines into the blue sky, although there was a single brownish-red leaf that clung on through wind and storms, like some remnant of a battle flag.

Laura looked forward to spring, when the branches would leaf out in green. She thought, A tree doesn't get made fun of for wearing the same leaves day after day. It's stupid not to be able to wear what you want to.

The days marched on. Fall gave way to winter, and one day it snowed. Laura sat at her desk. She looked out the window and said to the tree, "I'll throw snowballs up to you, and you can catch them."

This time everyone heard Laura because she had spoken out loud. The entire class burst out laughing.

"Laura," Miss Howl's piercing voice killed the laughter. "You will go and sit in Mrs. Morning's office until you can pay attention."

So poor Laura walked down the stairs and into Mrs. Morning's office. There was a smudge of ink on Mrs. Morning's nose, and her desk was a jumble of papers. "Laura, dear, what is it?" she asked kindly.

Before Laura could answer, there was a shatter-ing, and then a shout. Mr. Old appeared in the office, grasping the arm of a boy. Laura found herself star-ing at the boy. She had never seen him before—and yet wasn't there something familiar about him?

"He broke a window," said Mr. Old. "He threw a snowball at the window in the seventh-grade classroom. Deliberate vandalism."

"Now, now," said Mrs. Morning soothingly. "Let's not jump to conclusions." She turned to the boy. "You must be new here. I'm sorry. I don't remember your name."

"I'm Michael," said the boy. He was lanky, large-boned, and wearing a wool cap. He is cute, Laura thought, and when he smiled, little creases grew from the outside corners of his eyes.

"Well, then, Michael," said Mrs. Morning. "Tell us exactly what just happened. Throwing snowballs at windows is forbidden, you know," she added, a hint of laughter dancing in her voice.

"Deliberate," growled Mr. Old, who was enjoying himself thoroughly. He liked playing the part of a crusty old curmudgeon. "I watched him. Packed that snow in his hands, he did, took aim, and heaved."

"I did throw a snowball," said Michael. His voice was low, a little scratchy. "It feels so exciting to have hands and fingers and arms that can do things." His eyes were sparkling.

"Better go put a board in the window and find a broom to sweep up that broken glass," Mr. Old said, hiding a smile. "And no more snowballs," he added, shaking a finger at Michael.

But Michael wasn't looking at Mr. Old. He was looking at Laura. "It's so nice to see you up close," he said.

"Me?" asked Laura, flustered.

"Well, Michael, boys will be boys," Mrs. Morning said vaguely. "And now, I'd like the two of you to get back to your classroom."

"But—" said Laura. "I'm supposed to—"

"Come on, Laura," said Michael. He pushed her out of the office. "Show me where to go. I've been looking forward to this for so long."

With a little shiver skating up her back, Laura wondered how it was he knew her name.

"Take off your hat when you come into a building," Miss Howl snapped at Michael as he and Laura stepped into the room. Michael slowly pulled off his cap. The class turned and gasped. Michael had only one brownish-red tuft of hair on his head. Laura gazed at Michael. She turned to look out the window. The maple tree was no longer there.

"Now both of you sit down," commanded Miss Howl. "I've had enough interruptions for one day— what with girls who talk out loud in the middle of my classroom and windows that get broken. I hope you've learned your lesson, Laura."

Michael sat down in the empty desk next to Laura, the desk no one else ever wanted to sit in. Miss Howl stood sternly over Michael. "Who are you, young man? Why hasn't anyone told me there would be a new student in my class?"

"Oh!" Michael exclaimed, gazing up at Miss Howl. "You are Miss Howl, aren't you? I'm supposed to tell you something. Something about—something about who you are, or were, but . . . I just can't remember."

To everyone's surprise Miss Howl did not speak, but simply cocked her head to one side. The class of students sat utterly still, waiting to see what would happen. "Who was I?" she whispered. For a moment the lines in her face softened, and a ghost of a smile haunted her thin, hollow face. "You remind me of someone I used to know, but I can't think who," she said.

She turned to look out the window. Another second and she would have remembered, but someone (probably Marie) giggled. The moment was lost.

"Now then," said Miss Howl crossly, "take out your homework. You were to make a drawing of your family tree."

There was a rustling of papers, a snapping open of notebooks. Laura didn't move. She hadn't done her homework. Well, she had started to. She had put in her great-grandparents and grandparents. And her father and her mother. But her mother had been married three times. Miss Howl hadn't explained where on the diagram you were supposed to put all those extra stepfathers. And besides, did everyone have to know about that?

"Can I borrow some paper and a pencil?" Michael asked her.

Laura gave him paper and pencil, and then turned to look out the window again. But Mr. Old was there now, blocking her view, and what was worse, he was putting up a piece of plywood in the window where the glass used to be. Laura felt tears come into her eyes. What was she going to do if she couldn't see her tree?

Miss Howl was going from desk to desk. She stabbed a finger at Martin's paper. "Messy," she said. "Do it over."

Ooooh, Laura thought. What is Miss Howl going to say when she sees I haven't done anything? She shivered with worry, and then, curious, glanced over at what Michael was drawing. What kind of family did he come from? But his arm was in the way, and she couldn't see.

Then Michael raised his hand. "Do you want it with leaves or without, Miss Howl? You didn't say."

Miss Howl swooped over to him. She snatched up his paper and held it up high for all to see. It was a large maple tree, with lots of leaves, a bird sitting on its highest branch. The class giggled nervously, but Laura's heart turned over.

Now she knew who Michael was. She wouldn't

need to look out the window anymore to talk to her friend. He was sitting in the desk next to her.

Sunday, January 17

Boring, boring Saturday and Sunday.

Tuesday, January 19

I haven't seen Howie around lately. He hasn't come to his door when I've knocked. He hasn't been in the day students' lunchroom. I want to tell him I like the second story. I like Laura. I wish the maple tree could turn into a boy and be my friend.

The trouble is, I can't go prowling and talk to him at night because get this: Miss Hammer caught Bix Potter and Trudy Lockhart sneaking about at night, stealing food from the kitchen. Not even I would dare do that. Now the housemothers are on a rampage and are staying up all night prowling themselves, trying to catch kids.

To make things worse, Janie Parker started a fire in her closet because she studies in there after lights-out. She fell asleep, and the lamp fell against some clothes and burned them. It's lucky Janie woke up.

And then I guess Shirley Moss and Tracey Hartzog, who are juniors, saw some boys walking outside their window after lights-out. They yelled down to them, and the boys yelled back. Tracey, who had some firecrackers, chucked them out the window. Miss Birdie's room is right below theirs. She woke up and heard the firecrackers. She went bonkers, thinking it was an air raid. She had to be carted away. No more Miss Birdie.

Now that she's gone, I sort of feel sorry for her. Shirley and Tracey are in a lot of trouble because of having the firecrackers.

I'm glad other kids get into trouble. It makes me feel less bad.

Tonight I'm going to write about Christmas in Minneapolis with Mom. Mom's apartment is too small for a big tree so she got this little artificial Christmas tree. We decided we'd only put red things on it. We bought red bows, red balls, and little red birds. It actually was pretty. We went Christmas caroling with friends she's made in her neighborhood. It was kind of fun, but the people are weird. There is one guy who was singing next to me, and his breath was bad. It smelled like booze, and I didn't like him. Mom said he is a famous actor in Minneapolis. Mom gave me a book of Robert Frost poems, *Jane Eyre*, and a Kingston Trio record for Christmas. It is really *really* cold in Minnesota in the winter! Even colder than here, where it is ridiculously cold right now.

Wednesday, January 20

Howie was putting up new bulletin boards outside of the art room today. I stopped to talk to him.

"Where have you been?" I asked.

"Busy," he said. He was a drilling a hole, and it didn't seem as if he really wanted to talk to me.

It actually made me a little mad. I stamped my foot. "What does *busy* mean?" I asked.

Howie still didn't stop drilling. When he finally finished, he turned and said, "Now tell me, Lydia, what part of Australia are you from? Sydney? Perth? The Great Victoria Desert?"

"You're mad at me for lying," I said.

"No, I'm mad at you for saying 'What does busy mean' in that little tone of voice of yours. When I say I've been busy, I mean I've been busy."

I stared at Howie. To tell the truth, he didn't look all that great. He was rumpled, as if he'd been sleeping in his clothes; only he had dark circles under his eyes, as if he hadn't been to bed in a while. He looked like he needed a haircut, or a shave, or something. I felt a little stab of worry.

I took a deep breath and said, "I am not from Australia. I am from Hidden Lake, New Hampshire."

"Aha," he said.

"Can I read another Silly Wizard story?" I asked. I wanted him to look happier. "Does Miss Howl ever figure out she was an owl?"

"Do not spit against the wind, for obvious reasons," he said.

That was better, more like the old Howie.

"Howie, *please?*"

"What happened to your Silly Wizard task?"

"I'm actually working on it," I said, even though that isn't exactly true. I have kind of stopped thinking about it, waiting for Elizabeth Longford to write me back.

"Meet me at 4:35, pronto, at the entrance of the Silly Wizard's lair," he said.

Yeah, he was back to being himself now, but he did need a haircut. For the first time I wondered where he lives and if he lives alone. I get the feeling his wife isn't alive. Maybe he lives in the maintenance room.

Thursday, January 21

After dance I saw Howie eating supper in the day students' lunchroom so I sat with him and told him he should make the Silly Wizard stories into a book, illustrate it with his paintings, and get it published.

"Huh," he grunted.

I crossed my arms and held them tight against me. I felt like Miss Sparring when she is really cross. "Why not?" I asked.

He laughed. "It's not that easy to get published. They have to *like* what you send them."

"Of course they'll like it."

Howie laughed again. "So tell me what's new in your life?"

I knew he was changing the subject, but I didn't mind because I felt like telling him about the water clock and Miss Sparring. Howie is a very good person to tell things to. His eyes looked sad and serious while I was talking.

"Perhaps you could work on the water clock in your art class," he said.

"I guess," I said.

"What do you mean, you guess?"

"The other girls will make fun of me. And besides, I don't really think I can do it. It's too complicated."

"Well," said Howie. He thumped the table. "I could help. Lots of room right here for a project like that."

My heart leaped at the thought of Howie helping me make a water clock. But then I saw girls going by in the hallway and wondered: If they saw me working with the maintenance man on a project like this, would they make fun of me? Or would Miss Sparring find out I was still trying to make it and get mad?

Howie was looking at me. "It's on my own time," he said. "I'm not on duty right now, if that's what you're worried about."

I blushed. I hadn't been worried at all about him.

"We'll have to pick up after ourselves. We can store it under the stairs."

"It would be great," I said.

"So what are we going to need?"

I took a deep breath and started to describe how the water clock worked, and he said, "Hold on, Lydia, let's start with a drawing."

He cleared his plate away to make a space, and then pulled a crumpled piece of paper and a stubby pencil from his pocket and handed them to me. I drew him a diagram.

"That's fabulous," he said. "What a contraption. You know what? This reminds me. A few years ago somebody decided all the clocks in every classroom ought to be the same."

"Why?"

"Why, indeed," said Howie, shaking his head.

"It was probably Mr. O'Hare," I said. "He doesn't like it if the thumbtacks on his bulletin board aren't in a straight line."

Howie smiled and said, "At any rate, all the old clocks were removed so we actually have a closet full of perfectly functioning timepieces. Not pig hearts, but clocks! Come with me."

We went out into the hall, and he opened a door I hadn't noticed before. He opened it with a set of keys he had attached to his belt. It turned out to be a closet full of clocks! "Maybe we can use some spare parts for your water clock."

"Goodie," I said, and then it was time for me to go. But it was a pretty good day today because of that.

Friday, January 22

Today I asked Fish, "Have you ever noticed that all the clocks in the school are alike?" During recess he and I went from classroom to classroom checking it out. Sure enough, they are all the same.

"How'd you happen to notice that?" Fish asked.

"I'm very observant," I said.

Now I'm going to write about Gran's. When I used to lie in my bed at Hidden Lake and look out my window at night, a star was framed between two trees. I always made a wish on it, or maybe it was a prayer. When I was little I always said a prayer before going to sleep. I would say, "God bless Mom and Dad and Gran and Aunt Fay and Uncle Doug and Aunt Susie and Uncle Morris and cousin Michael." Then I'd list all the kids in my class at school and all my teachers and the man at the pharmacy who always gave me peppermints when we went in there, and last of all would be Jip and Benny the canary. I remember Benny died on Thanksgiving. That was the year

Gran roasted little game hens, so when she brought them out, I cried because I thought one of them was Benny.

I barely remember that happening, but it was one of Gran's favorite stories. Isn't it funny how you're not sure if you remember things that have happened to you when you are little, or if you think you remember because you've seen photographs, or you've been told the same story so many times you think you can remember?

Anyway, as I got older, sometimes I'd be too tired to say the whole list, so I'd say, "God bless everyone." I don't even know when I stopped saying that. But when I was lying in my bed at Hidden Lake, with Jip curled up next to me, I would look at my special star, and I'd feel safe and warm. So sometimes I'd say, "Thank you for me being here."

Saturday, January 23

I am going to write about Christmas with Dad-and-April.

Mom drove me to the airport so I could fly to Boston. I just stood in the waiting area and cried. Mom cried, too.

I wouldn't mind being with Dad so much if he still lived in our old house or if there were woods and kids in the neighborhood. But now he lives in that horrible town house in the city, where you can't touch anything.

No matter what I do there, April looks over my shoulder. I just try to stay in my room, but after a while I have to come out.

When I got to their house, we had to celebrate Christmas again. Because of the divorce, I have to celebrate Christmas twice. Their Christmas tree is a perfect Christmas tree, of course, with shiny balls and drippy, silvery icicles. April always brags about how she brought the ornaments back from Germany.

Dad put on the *Messiah* while I sat on the Oriental carpet and opened presents, and smelled rug cleaner and furniture polish mixed with Christmas-tree smell. April gave me a sweater and a scarf and mittens that she knit especially for me. *Guilt guilt guilt.* Dad gave me three records, one of Schubert, one of Brahms, and one of Mozart. I wondered if I should tell him Mom gave me the new Beatles record.

After we opened the presents, Dad and I went for a walk in the park. He is gray these days, foggy gray. His face is blurry, and he is far away; I can't talk to him. Music is the only thing he cares about, but only the right music. He shuts himself up in his room and plays the viola for hours. What is the point of beautiful music if you are going to be mean to people? He isn't interested in anyone unless they like what he likes.

I think he and Mom didn't get along because she likes Frank Sinatra and Bing Crosby and now the Beatles.

"How is school?" he asked, and I said, "Fine."

I couldn't say anything more. All the words I could say were swarming inside me like a bunch of angry bees. I could only let one word out at a time, so when I opened my mouth, just the word *fine* came out. It was the only word safe to let out; otherwise all the others would fly out and sting him to death. "How are the piano lessons going at school?" he asked. "Fine," I said. I didn't tell him the school had forgotten to arrange a piano teacher for me, and I hadn't reminded anyone. I hadn't had a single lesson in months.

I didn't tell him I didn't want to take piano lessons. Maybe because I hated my piano teacher, Mrs. Norma Clarke. When I was younger and we all still lived together, I used to have to go straight from school into Boston for my lessons. Sometimes I'd forget my piano books. Once Mrs. Clarke said, "If you forget your piano books one more time, I'm going to have to spank you." I felt myself get hot and worms crawled inside of me as I imagined her spanking me. I wanted to get up and run out of her apartment. Even when Mom moved away, and I was only spending half the year with Dad, I still had to take lessons from her. Mom doesn't have a piano, so I never practiced when I was with her. I never made any progress. Every time I went back to Boston it was like starting all over. Mrs. Norma Clarke didn't like working with me.

And then Dad said, "By the way, I have asked Mrs. Clarke to come over to give you a lesson."

My heart lurched and then stopped. I had to clutch my chest. Any normal person would have thrown themselves on the ground and screamed and cried. I can never act like that with Dad. Maybe that's why I'm especially wild at times with other people.

I want to write about the piano lesson, but I'm not sure where to start. Maybe I should describe Mrs. Norma Clarke. She has greasy black hair, and her face is pitty because I guess she had bad pimples when she was a kid. She tries to cover it up with cakey white makeup. Her mouth is a gash of red lipstick. She wears perfume that gets trapped in her tight black sweater. She has really bad breath.

On the day, she walked in the door, and Dad-and-April rushed to meet her. They oozed all over her because Mrs. Norma Clarke is a big deal in the music-teaching world. She acted really pleased to see me, although I know perfectly well she doesn't like me.

April said, "We'll just leave you two alone to get down to business."

Mrs. Clarke and I sat down at the piano, which was cluttered with photos of Dad-and-April on their wedding day. "What have you been working on?" Mrs. Clarke asked. I was going to tell her I hadn't practiced in a while. I actually started to, but her perfume and her bad breath made me not want to open my mouth. I was having trouble even breathing. I barely managed to start the Clementi, which was the last thing I had been working on a hundred years ago. I started to play, but my hands weren't connected to my brain. I saw them reflected on the piano just above the keys. They looked like two lumpy fish. Out of the corner of my eye, I could see Mrs. Clarke smiling in that fake way she has when she is impatient.

"We haven't practiced much, have we?" she said. Her voice was smarmy, which is a word Gran used to use when she was describing people she didn't like.

"No, *we* haven't," I said.

Mrs. Norma Clarke stiffened up. "Mother still doesn't have a piano?" she asked, even smarmier.

"If you mean my mother, no, she does not have a piano. Why should she?" I asked, feeling myself getting hot. I curled my hands into fists. "She doesn't have room in her house for a piano. And besides, I'm never with her, so what difference does it make?"

Mrs. Clarke sniffed. "I don't know why your father set this lesson up. I mean, really, if you haven't been practicing. And you don't really seem to care for this. It's a terrible waste of his money," she said.

"Yes it is," I said.

"Well," she said with a big sigh. "Do get on with it."

So I uncurled my hands and started playing again. I didn't care anymore how bad it was. I played for a while.

All of a sudden she stuck her arm right across my face, pointed to the music, and said, "Lydia, this is the fifth time you have missed the B-flat. I have been counting."

That's when I felt the pricks in my chest, and the black and white piano keys were all blurry and mixed up with Mrs. Norma Clarke's white face, her black sweater, and the white flecks of dandruff on her black sweater. All I could smell was her perfume and bad breath, and here was this dry flaky arm across my face. The next thing I knew, I bit her. Oh ugh ugh ugh. I can still feel her dry flaky skin in my mouth. She screamed, twisted around, and jabbed me in the back, and she kept screaming and screaming. Dad came rushing in with April close behind.

Mrs. Norma Clarke stood up from the piano bench and yelled, "She bit me, she bit me!"

I ran out of the room and out of the house. It was freezing out there, but I didn't care. I saw a taxi coming, so I stuck out my hand and waved it down. I got into the taxi and said, "I want to go to New Hampshire." The taxi driver swung around and looked at me and said, "*New Hampshire?* You gotta be crazy, girlie. I can't take you to New Hampshire."

"Please," I said, and I was beginning to cry.

"You running away or something?" he asked.

"I'm going to my grandmother's house. That's not running away," I said.

"I'd like to help you out, girlie, I really would; but I can't take you to New Hampshire. You can understand that, can't you?" He was really nice, actually, and that made me want to cry more; but I got out of his cab. He looked at me for a minute and said, "You sure you're gonna be all right, now, girlie? You have some place to go?" I nodded yes, and he reached out and patted me on the arm.

After he left I felt much calmer. Most of all, I was glad I had bitten Mrs. Norma Clarke. I started running, and then leaping. I ran saying, "No no no no," and then leaped, saying, "No more Mrs. Norma Clarke." Then I ran again, saying, "No no no," and leaped again and said, "No more piano lessons." I went for a long way doing this until I wasn't cold at all. Then I started running again and said, "No no no," and leaped and shouted, "No more Pocket School. *They can't make me go back there!*" And all of a sudden, there was Dad's car coming down the street.

He stopped the car, leaned over, and opened the door. He didn't say anything. I didn't know what to do, so I got in. He looked at me for a minute and still didn't say anything. Because he was so quiet, I couldn't say anything. I couldn't say a single thing I was planning to say, like I wasn't going back to Pocket or anything like that. And do you know what? We drove to the *movies*. Have you ever heard of anything so strange? I hardly ever go to the movies with my father. He hates movies. I could barely remember the last time I'd gone to a movie with him. I have never felt so strange in my life sitting next to him. The whole time he didn't say one word to me. Then we drove home, and still he didn't say anything. As we got closer to the house, I was beginning to feel shaky because by now I didn't want to face April. Dad unlocked the front door, and everything was quiet and dark. April was nowhere around. All Dad said was, "Good night, Lydia."

I went into my room. On my desk was some of April's stationery and a fountain pen. There was also an envelope with a stamp. "Mrs. Norma Clarke" was written on it in April's handwriting with Mrs. Clarke's address written underneath it.

And then a power took over my body. I sat down at the desk, picked up the fountain pen, and wrote: "Dear Mrs. Clarke, I am sorry I bit you. I don't know what came over me. I am very sorry if I hurt you. I think you are a very good piano teacher, and I am lucky to have someone like you teaching me. Sincerely, Lydia Rice."

I just remembered Fish calls fountain pens "blood pens." He says the ink in them reminds him of blood because it flows out so easily. Well, the letter I had to write to Mrs. Clarke was definitely written with my blood.

The power made me fold the letter, put it into the envelope, and lick the envelope shut. Then I climbed straight into bed and went to sleep. The next day the power made me walk to the mailbox and mail the letter.

After that I saw Dad-and-April, and they acted as if nothing had happened. I never got to tell them I didn't want to take piano lessons anymore. I never got to tell them I didn't want to go back to Pocket.

Sunday, January 24

Another boring Sunday.

Monday, January 25

Today we were supposed to sign up for the dance with our brother school. I am the only girl in my class who didn't sign up. You are supposed to put how tall you are next to your name so they can match you up with a boy who is taller than you. The short girls lie about how tall they are because they want tall boys. Collie came up to me and said, "I don't really blame you for not wanting to go to the dance." She makes me sick. She is only nice to me if the others aren't around.

I haven't seen Howie around. I want to read more of Silly Wizard.

I hate recess even more than ever now. Whitney, Collie, Weasle, and Ellie stand in the hallway and whisper and laugh. And no one wants to play outside anymore. I guess I don't even want to. It's freezing cold, and there's no place to play outside at Pocket during the winter. The snow in the courtyard is trampled down so it is hard and icy with ugly holes in it as if it has acne or something. It reminds me of Mrs. Norma Clarke's face. Oh well, anyway, I guess I am too old to play outside. Only little kids like winter.

Tuesday, January 26

It happened!! Today it happened! I got a letter from Elizabeth Longford!! It was typed and here it is.

Dear Lydia,

I am amazed and delighted to hear that the Pocket House mural is still there. I am the girl jumping rope, and I am tickled to learn that my nose has been rubbed away! I hope I have brought luck to many hundreds of Pocket girls!

And how clever of you to have hunted me down. How ever did you make that connection? I would love to tell you about Pocket in the old days, but the Second World War and a busy career following those long-ago school days have made me rather forgetful of details; however, I shall do the best I can.

We considered ourselves very lucky to study with Miss Pocket. She was such an accomplished woman with a simply splendid program for girls. The art, of course, was top class. Miss Pocket taught drawing, and there was a Miss Hammond who gave lessons in sculpture. Miss Hammond had studied in Italy, and there was a wonderful young man who did the painting. We were all, of course, terribly in love with him. He was simply magical to us, full of wisdom and wit. He was also an accomplished artist. He loved to tell stories, and he created the most wonderful illustrations to go with them. He would take us to museums. We'd stand in front of the paintings, and he'd ask us to make up stories about them. I've never forgotten a single painting because of that. I am sure I went on to become an illustrator myself because of his example. Mr. Pendragon, his name was. I have often wondered what became of him. So many times I have wanted to thank him for the encouragement he gave me.

As for the mural, there were five of us who rather fancied ourselves a gang, and several have remained my good friends for life. Abby Webb, for instance, who was the "best friend" in my book. She lives in Mills, you know—you could probably look her up. Then there was Connie Eisler who is the "Harriet" in the book. Did you know she is quite a famous photographer? She was a photojournalist during the war and won some awards. From time to time I see her work in *Life* magazine. Then there was Dottie—Dorothea Ehrenhaft—a lovely, serious girl, very intelligent. And finally there was Bunny Hamilton—mischievous and fun. Bunny was, perhaps, the best painter of us all. Do you know, I am not sure I ever did know her real name. She was called Bunny by teachers and students alike. I would love to know what she is doing now. Perhaps you can find out for me.

Pocket was such an exciting place to be for a girl in those days. We were not too often homesick, thinking it rather a lark to be away from home, but I do remember feeling a bit blue on Sunday evenings. Abby and I were roommates, and we cured the "wallows" as we called homesickness, by devising codes. We left messages in code for each other in the maple tree in the middle of the yard. There was a little hollow place down by the roots. I also remember that we wrote a play together called "The Pink Egg." We thought it brilliantly funny. How I would like to get my hands on that play now!

I did not know paring the entire peel could bring luck, but do you know that if you twist the stem of the apple as you say the alphabet, the letter you're on when the stem comes off, will be the name of your sweetheart?

Now, Lydia, do write back and tell me all about yourself, what you are doing, and what Pocket is like now.

With best wishes,
Elizabeth Longford

P.S. As for the letters in the border of the mural, I do remember about them. They are sort of a code, too. You were clever enough to track me down, so I bet you can puzzle out what they mean.

I had to wait all day to show Howie the letter. When I did, his face just lit up with the biggest smile. He read it once; he read it twice; he read it three times. He kept shaking his head and saying, "Amazing! That is really astonishing!" Then he grabbed my hand and shook it. "You are on your way, Lydia; you are really on your way."

"I've earned another Silly Wizard story," I said.

"Hmm . . . I suppose," he said.

He went into his lair and came back with an envelope. It is sort of fun reading a book like this, in installments. On my way up to my room, I stopped in the sitting room and picked up Elizabeth Longford's book. It was neat holding her book in one hand and Howie's "book" in the other.

And now it's lights-out, and my flashlight's on and I'm going to treat myself to reading the next chapter.

Susan, Once a Spider

One day the seventh graders were all at music. They were singing away, happy for the time being, not to be with Miss Howl. A spider, sitting in the dust in a crack between the floorboards, became so enchanted with Marie's singing (which was especially good) that she crawled up her leg so she could hear better. Marie, when she felt the crawling, screamed and brushed the spider roughly to the floor.

The poor spider lay stunned on the floor. When she regained consciousness, she realized that all she wanted in life was to be a girl who could sing. "I'll find a Silly Wizard," she said to herself.

She scuttered across the floor, up the wall, and swung herself out the window onto a slender but strong thread. Her journey was not an easy one, but finally she saw Mr. Old, walking across the courtyard, and realized he was a Silly Wizard.

"Wizard," she called out. In the stillness of the night, he could hear her tiny voice. "Wizard, I want to be a girl so I can sing."

Mr. Old paused in his rounds and stood beneath the moon, which was new now and getting stronger each day. "Let me see," he said, thoughtfully pulling on his beard. "I think I can remember that charm. It goes like this:

A song from the South,
A nose from the North,
Merry eyes from the East,
A wealth of black hair from the West."

"Is that all?" asked the spider. "You just chant the charm?"

"No," said Mr. Old. "You must molt. Seven times."

"All at once?" asked the spider.

"It must be done," said Mr. Old. "And spider, you must be a girl at this school. I need you to help Miss Howl remember who she was."

"All right," said the spider. When Mr. Old had finished explaining about Miss Howl, she began to molt.

With each layer she shed, the spider lost crawly legs and beady eyes; she gained girlishness and grew tall.

"Now sleep," said Mr. Old, "and when you awake, you will be Susan. I hope," he added under his breath, because Silly Wizards can never be exactly sure how their charms are going to come out.

Several days later Mrs. Morning was talking to Mr. Old. "That new girl, Susan, has a beautiful singing voice," she said.

"There's just one thing, though," he said, shaking his head. "Haven't you noticed? Whenever she begins to sing, all the spiders in the school come out to listen."

"Spiders?" Mrs. Morning asked, alarmed.

"Spiders," said Mr. Old, an odd gleam in his eye.

When Silas Smooth first saw Susan, he was undone. Love smote his freshly ironed chest.

Like a dog Silas followed Susan around school all day long. Sometimes he forgot to comb his hair. He scribbled hearts in the margins of his books. He forgot to turn his homework in.

At recess Susan sang and played the guitar, for that is what she most loved to do. Silas lay swooning at her feet. He adored her voice, and as Mr. Old had noted, so did the spiders. Perhaps there was some spiderness left in her voice that attracted them. In any case they crawled from everywhere to hear her sing.

One recess after an especially lovely song, Silas said, "Susan, you must marry me."

"Marry?" Susan replied. "But I'm only in seventh grade."

"I know exactly what I want in life," said Silas. "I am going to grow up, become a lawyer, marry you, and have two children, a boy and a girl."

Susan was rather flattered, but at that moment

Silas saw a spider. He squished it with a shiny shoe. Susan's brow darkened, and her eyes flashed. "Silas," she shouted, rising up, "I will *never* marry you! You just killed my sister or my cousin or my aunt, I don't know which; but I hate you, and I will never *never* marry you. I am going outside tonight and find the Silly Wizard and go away from you."

She burst into tears and flinging the guitar aside, ran off. Silas, of course, was amazed.

That night two figures stood beneath the moon. One was Susan, and one was Mr. Old. Silas waited nearby, in the shadow of the school building.

"Wizard," said Susan, "I'm ready to be a spider again."

"So soon?" asked Mr. Old. "Did you remember to speak to Miss Howl?"

"What was I supposed to tell Miss Howl?" asked Susan.

"Who she was," said Mr. Old, a trifle impatient. Why couldn't any of these transformed creatures remember anything?

"Please," said Susan. "I just want to be a spider again."

"I suppose you've lasted longer than I thought you would," said Mr. Old. "In the end spiders usually want to go home. Well, here's the charm:

"Gnat, moth, earwig, worm,
Girl to spider, now return."

Right before Silas's astonished eyes, Susan turned into a spider. She shrank rapidly, hair growing all over her, arms and legs multiplying and becoming crawly.

"O familiar dirt," cried Susan, now a spider. "I am so happy to be a spider again. I have so many legs to run and play with." She stopped speaking and sang notes, up and down the scale. Her voice was lovely still, as rich and mellow, as perfect in its pitch as it had been when she was Susan. "O Wizard!" she called out happily. "What a wonderful wizard you are! You turned me back into a spider, but you let me keep my human voice."

"No trouble at all," said Mr. Old, rather pleased, as he had had no idea that this was going to happen.

"But what about me?" cried Silas, leaping out from the shadows. "What is going to happen to me if Susan is no longer in my life? O Wizard, king of the night," he said, bending on one knee, "I want to be a spider, too."

Mr. Old stepped back in surprise. "No one wants to be a spider. Except people who used to be spiders."

"I do," said Silas. "I want to be a spider so I can be with Susan." He knelt down, muddying the knees of his crisp, clean trousers. "Susan, where are you?"

Mr. Old felt sorry for the lovesick boy. He began to chant the charm:

"Small size from the South,
New legs from the North,

Eight eyes from the East,
A web from the West."

"Now you must curl yourself up into a ball."

Silas swallowed nervously and tucked his head between his knees. And then he began to shrivel. Mr. Old waited for him to change shape, but all that happened was that he grew small. He was Silas Smooth in miniature, still wearing a jacket, tie, trousers, and shiny shoes. Mr. Old groaned slightly, and shook his head.

Susan hurried over to him. "Silas," she exclaimed.

"Susan," he said, uncurling and standing up. He looked down at himself. "What has happened to me?"

"Silas," said Susan. "You must ask that Silly Wizard to change you back. This is no life for you."

"But Susan," said Silas miserably, "I want to be with you. Won't you change yourself back to a girl? I promise I won't ever step on a spider again."

"No," said Susan. "I wanted to be a girl because I loved the sound of the human voice. But I was homesick as a girl." She rubbed two hairy legs together. "Now I have the best of both worlds, although I was beginning to like playing the guitar, and that, of course, is no longer possible."

Miniature Silas sat on a stone and tried to think. "I can see that being a small human in your world could be unpleasant," he said. "A bird could come along and peck me to death. Or I could easily be trapped in a spider's web." He shuddered at the thought. "No, this isn't going to work at all. I will have to ask the Silly Wizard to change me back."

He was just about to call out to Mr. Old when Susan began to sing. And as she sang, she spun her web. She sang a lovely, peaceful song, full of the contentment she felt at being home again.

Silas was inspired to do a wonderful thing. He stood up from the stone. From tiny twigs he fashioned a tiny harp, stringing it with spider's threads. Susan was so happy she embraced him with all of her legs. And then she began to sing and play.

Silas sat down again and listened. It was a beautiful, delicate, intricate sound, her pure, sweet voice blending with the harp.

Mr. Old leaned against a tree and closed his eyes and smiled.

When Susan finished her song, Silas stood up and said, "It is time for me to go now, Susan. Wizard," he called, "make me a boy again."

"Must you leave now?" Susan asked sadly. "Wait a little longer before going back. There is so much about my world I want to show you."

So for the next few days, Susan took Silas sightseeing. They watched carpenter ants being born in an old log; they investigated, at a distance, a bees' nest. The queen bee even came out and chatted with them for a while. Silas met other spiders, some who swam in water, some who made webby tents for houses on blades of grass. One night he even went to a concert given by crickets. It was all so interesting and exciting, Silas almost didn't want to leave.

"But you know you must," said Susan.

"Yes," said Silas.

On the third night he asked the Silly Wizard to change him back. Mr. Old cleared his throat and intoned:

"Much taller than spiders are most men;
Make Silas be himself again."

Just as Silas shot up to his full height, Susan screamed out, "Silas, wait! I remember who Miss Howl was! You must tell her!" But Susan was too late. Silas was busy jumping around, making sure that everything was working properly. He ran joyously around the courtyard because now he really knew what he was destined to be in life—not a lawyer at all, but an entomologist.

People at the school did wonder where Silas and Susan had been, and why Susan never returned; but Silly Wizard magic is quick to muddle memory. It wasn't long before no one wondered anything at all.

Silas turned up in blue jeans, sneakers, and an

old shirt, his tails untucked, his hair awry. He longed, always, to be outside. His worried parents came in for conferences as his grades fell from A's to C's.

The plague of pranks had ended. Miss Howl took credit for the change. "I am a good teacher," she often said to herself. She became even stricter, meaner, scarier.

Wednesday, January 27

I was so tired today. I can tell Lacey is sick of trying to wake me up every morning. I keep falling asleep in math class. Math is a hopeless situation anyway. Everyone is much smarter in the class than I am. Except for maybe Ginny Pearson, who sits there and pulls her hair out. She pulls at the top of her scalp and yanks out one hair at a time. She is beginning to have a bald spot.

Miss Harmony doesn't think I try, but I do. I just get distracted. Like today Miss Harmony was talking about a four-sided pyramid and how to find its surface area. All I could think about was I never knew a pyramid could have four sides. I thought it only had three, so I said so out loud. Miss Harmony said, "Shh, Lydia, don't interrupt."

"Can a pyramid have any number of sides?" I asked; but Miss Harmony said, "That is beside the point."

I said, "It is beside the point, the point of the pyramid, get it?" But no one laughed. Whitney and Collie, of course, looked disgusted, and Miss Harmony sighed and said, "Lydia." I sat and tried to draw a four-sided pyramid with the broken lines, you know, for the base. But when I tried to count if it had four sides, my eyes jumped around. I couldn't tell which was the base and what were the sides.

Miss Harmony has braids wrapped around her head, and she wears flowered blouses with round collars. She has freckles. She looks like an eleven-year-old fifty-year-old, or is it a fifty-year-old eleven-year-old? She is so old-young looking. She nods and bobs her head a lot. She likes smart girls, and smart girls like her. She *loves* Fish because he is so good in math, and I think she is so happy to be teaching a *boy*.

At supper tonight Fish said, "The Egyptian pyramids have four sides."

"Why didn't you tell me that in class?" I asked.

"Because that would have been getting off the subject," he said. Then he said, "Did you know if you went up in space, you wouldn't see your reflection in a mirror?"

Talk about getting off the subject.

Since he knows so much, I asked him, "What is an entomologist?"

"Someone who studies insects," he said right away, just like that.

"Oh, of course," I said. "That makes sense."

"What makes sense?"

"I read a story about a boy who hated spiders, and then he fell in love with a girl who used to be a spider but who was turned into a girl. Then she was turned back into a spider, and he got turned into a miniature person and hung around with her, the spider who used to be a girl. When he turned back to his regular size again, he wanted to be an entomologist."

"Sounds like a great story," said Fish, rolling his eyes.

"It *is* a great story," I said. "You should read it."

I worked on the water clock with Howie today. And guess what? He got his hair cut and trimmed his beard. He looks younger. He was wearing a new shirt. It smelled new and looked new. It was all creased and sharp-looking.

"You look nice," I said.

"I thank you," said Howie.

"Is Miss Howl going to remember she was an owl?" I asked.

"It depends on whether or not I ever get around to figuring it out," he said.

"You have to," I said.

Thursday, January 28

Tonight has to be one of the worst I've had at Pocket yet.

We had mystery meat for supper. And beets! Slimy, disgusting beets. And smashed potatoes. That's what Whitney calls them. "Pass the smashed potatoes," she said. I laughed, and she asked, "What are you laughing about?" And I said, "It just sounds funny, smashed potatoes. I've always called them mashed potatoes."

Whitney pressed her lips together and turned about the same red as the beets. Then she said, "I thought you were taking dance."

I said, "I am."

"Then how come you're never there?" she asked. Now it was my turn to start turning red. "Ellie Peterson says you're never there. Ellie says you spend the whole dance class behind the curtain on the stage." I didn't say anything. Everyone at the table was looking at me now, including Mrs. Fisk.

Fish piped up: "Hey, Whitney, maybe you should stand

up and make an announcement to the whole dining room. Anyway, Whitney, how are you going to prove it?"

Fish's voice got even louder than usual. I thought for a minute he was going to get up and punch Whitney. He was acting like my friend. Or like my lawyer. I wasn't sure which. "And aren't you the one I saw on Blakeley Street the other day?"

Whitney looked as if the smashed potatoes didn't agree with her. Blakeley Street is off-bounds. Only seniors with permission are allowed to go there. There's a record store and a diner that's a teenage hangout. It is considered dangerous and not ladylike for Pocket girls. So Whitney didn't say another word. But when Mrs. Fisk was excusing us, she said, "Lydia, stay a moment, please."

Everyone left. I sat at the table and stared at the salt and pepper shakers. "I don't care how much trouble I get into because I am going to be a Silly Wizard," I said to myself.

"Lydia," she began. That's how they always begin. Lydia, Lydia, Lydia. "Lydia, do you think you can get yourself to stop skipping out of your dance class?"

"I suppose so," I said.

"Well, if you promise me you can, then I promise you I will keep this under my hat." I flicked a look at her. "This could be very serious, you know, Lydia. You could be sent home."

A little thrill went through me. Here was the answer: Get into wicked trouble and get sent home. But then I thought, which home? Mom's little apartment that is really hot in the winter and has a funny smell because the Chinese restaurant across the street blows all its kitchen smells into the apartment? Or would they send me to Dad-and-April's? Then I'd get the silent treatment like I did when I bit Mrs. Norma Clarke. I couldn't live through something like that again. I don't even want to go there during the long weekend that's coming up.

I thought, If I leave Pocket, I'll miss Howie, and I'll never find out what happens next in his story. Or finish my water clock. Or finish my task.

"So is it a deal, Lydia?" she asked.

It slowly sank into my brain that she was saving me. I couldn't think of anyone else at Pocket who would let me get away with skipping out of dance class. "Mrs. Fisk," I asked, "why are you being so nice?"

She fiddled a little with the salt and pepper shakers. Then she put a hand on my arm. "We have been at this school five years, and you are the first real friend Alexander has made since he's been here." I swallowed hard because I didn't think I was much of a friend to Fish. "The least I can do is be kind to you."

I squeezed out a weak thank you. The whole conversation was embarrassing.

"Now, are you going to attend that dance class?" she asked sternly.

I sighed. I couldn't quite say yes. She patted my arm again. "What's the trouble, Lydia?"

"Do you have to give me an IQ test?" I finally managed to get it out.

"Oh!" she said, looking startled.

"I will go to dance class if you promise you won't give me an IQ test."

Mrs. Fisk shook her head. "You're a tough customer, Lydia. I don't know if I can make such a promise. It's required, you know."

"But I'll flunk it," I said.

Mrs. Fisk frowned. "Tell you what, Lydia. We won't think about that test for a while. I can always give it to you next year."

I thought, Yeah, but there's not going to be a next year.

"Are you all right, dear?" She put a hand on my shoulder, and I thought she seemed soft and pillowy. I wanted to lean into her for a minute because no one ever hugs you at boarding school.

"Yes," I said. I thought, Nope, there's not going be a next year. Not if I can help it.

Friday, January 29

Yesterday I was supposed to work on the clock with Howie, but he wasn't in the lunchroom. I knocked on his door. No answer. I don't know why, but I had a feeling he was in there and just wasn't answering. I banged on the door with my fist. Sure enough, out he came.

"What are you doing, Lydia?" he asked.

"What's the matter with you? How come you look so glum?"

"Glum?" He actually smiled. "Glum does not seem like a word a girl your age in this part of the century would be using."

"It's one of Gran's words. That, and smarmy. When she didn't like someone, she said they were smarmy."

"I'm sure I would like your grandmother."

I blushed. I had forgotten that I'd lied to Howie about her. "You would have liked her. She's dead."

Howie's head kind of snapped back. "Oh!" he said. "I didn't know. Gee whiz, I'm really sorry to hear that. How long ago did she die?"

"Two years ago," I said.

He sighed and pulled on his beard. "Let's go sit down," he said. "Sorry about the clock. We can work on that another day, okay?"

"Yes, it's okay," I said, following him down the hall. "I just think you're mad at me sometimes, and I don't get why."

We sat down on a bench in the lunchroom. Fish went by and poked his head in and shouted, "Hi, Lydia, hi, Howie," and then kept going.

"I like that boy," said Howie.

"He's okay," I said. "He's better than most of the girls around here."

"Yes, well, girls your age can be gruesome. But listen, Lydia, I'm not mad at you. You mustn't think when I get the way I get sometimes, it's because of you."

"Glum and gloomy," I said.

"It's hard to lose someone you love," he said. "Like your grandmother."

The instant he said that a picture jumped into my mind, the framed photograph of the pretty woman I had seen on his desk. "Like your wife?" I asked.

"Yes," he said. "How did you know?"

"I didn't really know. I guessed. That's crummy. I'm sorry she died."

Howie nodded, pressed his lips together, and didn't say anything. Two older girls passed by and asked if we'd seen one of their friends. I shook my head and said no. Howie stood up, patted me on the shoulder, and asked, "So how's the task coming along?"

"Okay," I lied. What I should have said was, "I'm kind of stuck, actually."

"You'll get it," he said. "But I'm going now. *Rach manji.*"

"*Naji, naji,*" I said.

On my way down the hall, I stopped and stood in front of the mural for a while. You could tell those girls were friends, all having a good time. You could tell none of them were mean like Whitney or Collie or Weasle or Ellie, acting as if they were old and sophisticated. I looked at each one of them closely.

The girl painting the picture has braids like the jump-rope girl but not as long. She's the one who ended up being the photographer. The girl reading seems, I don't know, peaceful. The girl who is sitting with the kitten in her lap seems a little, I guess the word is *plump*, like Nancy Drew's friend Bess is plump, not fat. It's funny, but now I remember that *plump* was also one of Gran's words. She would never have called someone fat. The plump girl is living here in Mills somewhere.

The girl who is in the tree has short yellow hair like me. I wonder where she is now and what she is like.

I wish I had been at Pocket back whenever it was. I

think the Pocket girls would have been my friends. I asked them, "What does A–B–C–D–E WHEEL mean?"

I traced the P in the bottom corner. I tried to imagine Miss Pocket standing here in this hallway, painting the mural.

As I turned to go up the stairs, I had this really odd feeling that they were all watching over me.

Saturday, January 30

I got a letter from Mom today.

She sent me one of her poems. It makes me feel so dumb because I don't understand it *at all*.

After dance class, and *yes* I have been going to my detestable dance class, I stopped by and showed the poem to Howie. He said he didn't understand it, either. That made me feel better, but he did say Mom must be a very smart woman.

Tonight, maybe because of Mom's letter, I have been thinking about how we used to be a normal family before Mom went out to Minnesota.

She went to be with her parents because they were getting old. She was worried about them. We thought she was only going for a little while, but she kept staying on and on. It was horrible. I hated that. Dad didn't seem able to cope. We hardly ate, and the house was always a mess. And he was *so* grumpy.

That's when Gran came down from her house in New Hampshire and stayed with us. She made delicious stews and was good at soups, too. She played Monopoly with me, and Crazy Eights and Chinese Checkers. She even read to me at night. *Winnie the Pooh* is what I remember the best. We laughed a lot about Eeyore because he was always so grumpy, and once she said, "Your father reminds me of Eeyore."

Gran helped me with my homework. That was when I liked school. It was this small school, and I could walk to it. We had Mr. Kellogg who was always assigning neat projects. I remember once I had to build the Wright brothers' airplane. And once I made a windmill. Gran helped me with both those projects. I think that's why I like the water clock so much—because of Mr. Kellogg and Gran. One thing I also remember from the time Gran stayed with us was that she took me to the Museum of Fine Arts in Boston. We stopped in front of the paintings and made up stories about them. I think I will always remember the paintings we looked at because of that.

Oh! That's so strange! I just realized that's what Elizabeth Longford said Mr. Pendragon used to make them do!

Anyway, then it was summer, and Mom was still away.

I remember when I realized it had been one hundred days since I had seen her.

Dad went out to Minnesota to be with her, so Gran and I went up to New Hampshire to Gran's house. I remember how glad Gran was to be home. It was early summer, and she kept walking around saying hello to flowers and hugging trees she had missed.

During that time Gran and I painted together. We'd pick a bunch of wildflowers and put them into a vase. We set them on a table, and we'd both try to paint them.

Halfway through the summer, Mom's dad died; then a few weeks later, her mother died. I went out to Minnesota for the funerals. It was strange because I had never known those grandparents very well. And it was also strange because it was such a sad time when I finally got to see Mom. She was *so* sad and really tired. I wasn't sure she was glad to see me. But when all the funeral stuff died down, Dad went back home, and Mom and I went looking for an apartment for her because she said she was going to stay out there for a while. We had the best time together, and I forgot all about how she had been gone for so long.

One funny thing I remember about that summer: Mom made me a peanut-butter-and-jelly sandwich every day for lunch. And every day she took a bite out of it before giving it to me.

When the summer was almost over, Mom asked if I

would like to live with her and go to school in Minnesota. At first I didn't understand because she didn't really explain it to me. I thought it would be all of us living there. I said something like, "What is Dad going to do?" And she asked, "What do you mean?" "For a job?" I asked. She said, "Why, what he *has* been doing, working as a chemical engineer." I asked, confused, "Here?" And she said, "No, in Boston." I asked, "How can he do that and live here?" Mom sat down then and said, "Oh, I thought you understood." Only then did I understand—and my skin felt too tight, and my bones felt watery.

It is hard writing this. I think this is the first time I've put down on paper everything that happened.

Well, I did stay with Mom and went to the big public middle school. At first I missed my old friends a lot and my old school. I had never been to a public school before, and there were *so* many kids! Mom wasn't working yet so it was before she knew anybody, either. The teachers at the school weren't anywhere near as good as Mr. Kellogg, but after a while I found out the kids were friendly. Pretty soon it got to be fun, and I didn't have as much homework as I used to have back home.

Then they told me I was going to go back east for Thanksgiving. And that I was going to stay with Dad for the rest of the school year. That's also when they told me Dad was selling our old house, and he was going to go live in a new place.

We had Thanksgiving with Gran. I remember zooming out of the car and running to the trees in front of her house and throwing my arms around them. The pine needles were like a soft carpet on the ground, and everything smelled so good. Then I ran and threw my arms around Gran. And then around Jip.

That was when I met April and found out Dad-and-April were going to get married.

That Thanksgiving was the last time I saw Gran and Jip.

And now I can't write anymore.

Sunday, January 31

Mrs. Fisk invited me to come have supper with her and Fish two nights from now when she is off duty. Wow! A meal that isn't Pocket food. Miss Sparring said I could go if I got all my homework done, so I guess I will try to do that. Good-bye. I have to go to work. Aaaaagh.

Monday, February 1

I had a science test today, and you know what, diary, I think I did pretty well. We are studying simple machinery, like levers and things, and I like that stuff a lot. I think Miss Copper likes me, too. She said I didn't just memorize the facts, but that I thought about them, and that kind of person makes a good scientist.

It feels good to write this. I am glad Gran gave me this diary.

Tuesday, February 2

I told Howie about Weasle, Ellie, and Collie, how they used to be my friends, but now they are mean. He said, "When attacked, become a cork bobbing on water. Then not even the sharpest sword can hurt you. Want to practice?"

"Practice? How?"

"Okay, attack me. Say something mean to me."

"Do I have to?"

"Come on, you'll only get good at this if you practice. Tell me I'm ugly or something."

"Okay," I said. "You're ugly."

Howie grinned and said, "Oh my, that is a very nice pair of shoes you are wearing, very very stylish."

"Huh?"

"See, I come bobbing back like a cork and throw you off guard. Try another insult."

"You're stupid," I said.

"Oh," he said, yawning and looking bored, "I see the snow has stopped."

I shook my head. "I don't know, Howie. I don't know if it'll work. Those girls make me weak."

"If you are not the lead dog," he said, "the view never changes."

"What do you mean?" I asked.

"With sled dogs there's always one dog who leads the others. She is out in front so she gets to see what's coming. The others who are behind can only see the back ends of other dogs. They don't have to think or make any decisions. They just follow the lead dog. Right now you're just looking at the back ends of those girls instead of thinking about where *you* might want to be going. And that surprises me because that's not the Lydia I know."

I am trying to think about all of that.

Thursday, February 4

I thought it was just going to be me who was invited to supper at Mrs. Fisk's, but Lacey was invited, too. Fish said his mother said it would make Lacey feel bad if it were just me.

Fish lives in Corner House, the old house between

Duckworth and Pocket Hall. We walked into the front hallway, and right away I was hit by an old wooden house smell. It made me think of Gran's house. There were winter coats heaped in a pile on a bench and boots lined up underneath the bench. I looked at Fish. "You are so lucky," I said.

"Why?" he asked.

"You live in a real house."

"Oh, yes, it *is* lucky to live in a house with ten stuck-up girls and a boring history teacher who wants to marry my mother."

"Mr. O'Hare does?" I asked, shocked.

"They go out," he said. "Didn't you know that? Everyone else in the school knows about it."

"Oh," I said, feeling really sorry for him. Lacey and I exchanged looks. I couldn't imagine anything more awful.

"Haven't you ever noticed how he tries to act like my father?" Then he grinned at me the way he always does, that stupid grin with the dimples, and he crossed his eyes.

At that moment Mrs. Fisk came out of a door and said, "Oh, hello. Why are you all hanging about in the hall? Do bring your guests in, Alexander."

I looked at Mrs. Fisk with new eyes. I tried to imagine her going out to a movie with Mr. O'Hare. Maybe the two of them held hands. You know what I think? It's positively repulsive. Even April is better than Mr. O'Hare.

We had stew and homemade bread for supper, and it was delicious; Mrs. Fisk treated Lacey like royalty and hardly paid any attention to Fish and me. This is the way everyone treats Lacey. And Lacey acted like royalty, saying "Please" and "Thank you" and "This is delicious" in that southern accent of hers. It's awful to be such a jealous person, but I am.

But then Fish started teasing Lacey instead of treating her like a dainty doll. He told her to chew with her mouth shut and to stop eating like a pig, which is ridiculous because Lacey picks and nibbles. Fish is the one who eats like a pig. He imitated her southern accent, saying things like, "Y'all pass the butter now." And it was a miracle because all of a sudden Lacey started to giggle. I don't think I have ever heard her laugh before. At the end of the meal, Mrs. Fisk said, "Alexander, you can clear the table and do the dishes."

Fish said, "Lacey and Lydia, y'all can clear and do the dishes cuz that's woman's work." Mrs. Fisk said, "Alexander!"

We all helped, although mostly Fish tried to snap us with his dish towel. He nearly hit his mother in the face. "Honestly, Alexander," Mrs. Fisk said. She had us sit at the kitchen table to do our homework. At first I was nervous. I wasn't used to doing homework like this, but with Lacey and Fish both sitting and working away, I knew I had to do something. To my surprise, Mrs. Fish said, "Lydia, let me help you with your math. I know you have trouble with math."

I wondered how she knew, and then I remembered the faculty meetings. Mrs. Fisk probably knows every single bad thing about me; and yet here she is, inviting me over to her house and everything. She helped me a lot, actually, and I understood how to find the stupid areas of all those stupid polygons for the first time. She explains things, which is more than Miss Harmony does.

It is too bad about Mr. O'Hare because when all is said and done, I think Mrs. Fisk is pretty nice.

We worked for a while. It felt like torture, actually, because I am not used to sitting still for that long and concentrating on homework. Finally Mrs. Fisk said, "That's enough for now."

"Let's go sledding," Fish suggested.

"Sledding?" Lacey asked quaveringly, as she is from the South where it doesn't snow. Fish asked, "You mean you've never been sledding?"

We piled on boots, coats, hats, and mittens. (Mrs. Fisk has collected lots of stuff like that after years of living with girls.) Fish got his sled, and we walked together, pulling it down the street. It was amazing to be walking around at night. There was a full moon, and the stars were out. I kept gulping air and feeling it across my face.

When we came to a tree, I threw my arms around it and said, "Hello tree, do you know me? I'm Lydia." I rubbed my cheek against its bark. Lacey laughed like anything. Then we came to the sledding hill.

Since there was only one sled, the three of us piled on and went down, me in front because I am the smallest, then Lacey, and then Fish who didn't really fit. He fell off halfway down and yelled, "Hey, Lacey pushed me off." She yelled, "I did not." I have never heard Lacey even raise her voice before.

We decided we would each take a turn going down alone. When it was my turn, I felt the air again, rushing by my face. I am free, I am free, I am free, I kept saying to myself as I went down.

At the bottom, I lay back on the sled and looked up. The moon was so big. It was saying, "Don't be homesick, Lydia. I am looking down on you and also on your mother."

I thought it must be a perfect moon for a Silly Wizard and realized it had been a month since I had met Howie. Only a month? It feels as if I have known him forever. Then all of a sudden Fish and Lacey jumped on me and scared me out of my mind. I had been so busy looking at the moon and thinking about Howie, I didn't even hear them sneaking up on me. Fish said we had to go back. Lacey sat on the sled, and Fish and I pulled her.

Mrs. Fisk's kitchen was warm and cozy. She made us hot chocolate with marshmallows and kept saying how rosy and healthy Lacey looked.

Then it was time for us to go back to Pocket House. When Lacey and I got back to our room, Mrs. Prokopovich stuck her head in and asked, "Have a good time, ducks?"

Lacey said, "Yes, thank you."

Mrs. P. said, "Well, ducks, it's lights-out then." When she closed the door, Lacey and I looked at each other, and Lacey, very quietly and without any expression, said, "Quackquack." We both burst out laughing and kept on laughing until I fell off the bed because I was laughing so hard.

The door opened, and Mrs. P. poked her head back in. "Now, ducks, it's time to settle down," she said, which only made us laugh even more. I thought I was going to die of laughter, and every time I caught Lacey's eye it got even worse. Finally Miss Sparring stormed in, turned off our light, and said, "One more sound out of you, hem-hem, and you will never go out to dinner again."

That shut us up.

Lacey is asleep now, and I am writing under the covers with my flashlight. It is the first time since I have been back from Christmas vacation that I have finished all of my homework. And even better, I have good food in my stomach.

I like Mrs. Fish. Fisk, I mean.

And guess what! I like Fish, Lacey, and, of course, Howie. And Elizabeth Longford. Good night, good night, good night.

Friday, February 5

There was a glee club concert tonight. Singing. Dad wanted me to join the glee club, but it is only for ninth through twelfth graders. So Lacey, Fish, and I aren't in it. I don't know if Fish could be in it, being a boy, but we were supposed to go and be in the audience. Instead we snuck backstage.

Everyone who was singing in the concert was standing in front of the curtains, which were shut, so we could run around on the stage behind them without being seen. Lacey and I danced, leaps and pirouettes; Fish ran like a madman in and out of the wings. Some of the kids' rear ends dented into the curtains. It was very tempting to poke them. When the singing began, we pretended we were singing, too. It was a lot of fun.

Sunday, February 7

Today was the best Sunday I have ever had at Pocket.

Every Sunday we have to go to church. Afterward, we have Sunday dinner, and then do nothing for hours and hours. Late in the afternoon we do homework (ha, that's a laugh) and have a disgusting "pickup" meal for supper. In the evening we meet in the sitting room for vespers. We sing hymns, and Mr. Wing or Miss Sparring or Mr. O'Hare say meaningful things. Later we have quiet hour and do nothing until we go to bed. But today, Sunday turned into one of the *best* days.

Fish and I decided to go to the Catholic church with Lacey. Usually I go to the Unitarian church because Dad-and-April want me to. Fish goes to the Episcopal church, but he said he wanted to broaden his religious experience. I think he just has a wicked crush on Lacey. Anyhow, I said I would go, too.

They get up and down a lot in the Catholic church. Fish said he liked it, but I felt stuffed by the end of it. I mean stuffed with incense and kneeling and sitting still. What is worse, at Pocket you have to wear stockings, gloves, a good coat, and a hat. Talk about being stuffed.

When they finally let us out, all I could do was breathe. The air was frosty and sort of damp. It felt as if there might be a big snowstorm coming. The frostiness stung my cheeks and the inside of my nose, and cleared church right out of my lungs.

On Sundays they let us walk to and from church. The walking back to school is the best part because you feel free for a short time. I like some of the streets of Mills, Massachusetts. The sidewalks are wide, and there are big trees and big houses with porches. I feel like a normal kid when I walk along them instead of a kid stuffed into boarding school. Today I especially didn't want to get back to school right away. I said, "Let's explore a little."

"We can't go out of bounds and besides, I'm freezing," said Lacey. I forgot she doesn't have blood in her veins, only water. Maybe if she ran around a bit, some of the water might turn to blood.

"We just can't go to Blakeley Street," I argued. "They didn't say we couldn't go other places."

There was this little narrow, twisty dark alley right where we were standing, and I darted into it. "Come on," I said. I ran down the alley, not even caring if Lacey and Fish were following. I'd go by myself if I had to, but Fish grabbed Lacey and pulled her along. The alley came out into another world, into a street with cobblestones, no cars, and old-fashioned lampposts. It was quiet, and there were three pretty stores lined up in a row—a Book Shoppe, an Antique Shoppe, and a Tea Shoppe. A shaft of sunlight was shining on the Tea Shoppe.

Oops. I just wrote that and now I realize that's impossible because it had begun to snow so there couldn't have been sun. But in my mind it was like that.

I was drawn by an invisible hand to the Tea Shoppe window. Before my eyes was a beautiful vision of tea cakes, little rectangles of creamy white with chocolate squiggles; little chocolate-covered squares with pink, green, and yellow squiggles; round cupcakes with globs of chocolate with red cherries on top; and eclairs, my favorite, with custard oozing out of them.

Fish and Lacey came over and stood beside me. "Look at that," I said. "I have money. I didn't put it all into the collection plate."

"We can't go in there," said Lacey. I looked at her. Her nose was red from the cold. All her blood was in her nose.

"We'll just go in for a minute," I said.

I opened the door. A cozy, warm, delicious sweet smell wrapped around us. There were three round tables with snappy white tablecloths on them. At one of the tables, an old lady was having tea by herself.

"We are going to have a tea party," I said and sat

down at one of the tables. Fish stood behind a chair and motioned for Lacey to sit down.

"Madame," he said.

"We can't," she said.

"Madame," he said again.

I could see the old lady was watching us. She caught my eye and smiled. It was the best smile I have ever seen in my life. Her entire face smiled.

Then a dried-up pruny kind of woman with slouchy shoulders came out in a black dress and a white apron. "Can I help you?" she asked in a sniffly voice. I looked over at the old lady. I thought she nodded as if to encourage me.

"Tea," I said. I thought about how April would say it. I stood straight and cleared my throat. "We would like a pot of tea and three cups, please, and a tray of napoleons, petit fours, eclairs, and cupcakes."

The woman stared straight ahead, no smile or anything. I wondered if I was making her work too much; then I could see the old lady watching, and she nodded again as if I had just done the best thing in the world.

Lacey and Fish sat down as if hypnotized. "Where'd you learn to act like that?" Fish asked.

"It's just something I know," I said. I sat and stuck my chin in the air.

"Petit fours, blah blah," said Fish in his loud voice. I winced.

"Keep your voice down," I snarled at him. "You don't want to be yelling in a place like this."

Out of the corner of my eye, I kept looking at the lady with the smile. She had straight white hair cut to her chin, clipped on both sides with a bobby pin that made her look sort of schoolgirlish. There were brown spots like big freckles all over her face that made her look friendly. Somewhere along the way in her life, she had lost a lot of her neck, and she was on the large size. Plump. She was wearing a big flowery dress and reminded me of a meadow.

The waitress shuffled over to our table with a pot of steaming tea and set it down. She sniffled and sighed. She went away and came back with cream and sugar. She went away again and came back with a silver platter full of the goodies. She put them down next to me as if I were in charge, even though she sniffled and sighed again. I felt very grand. I can see why April likes being in charge.

"Put your napkins on your laps," I said to Lacey and Fish, who were staring at the cakes.

"Isn't it in your lap, not on your lap?" asked Fish.

At the exact same moment, the three of us shook out the snappy white napkins that were sitting on the table in front of us. Just doing that made Lacey giggle. Our eyes met, and it was all over. Lacey and I could not stop laughing. We knew we had to be quiet, so we kept trying to stuff the laughter back inside of ourselves. Fish's eyes got very goggly, and every now and then he'd ask, "What is so funny?" The sniffly waitress was slouching in the corner without any expression on her face and that only made me laugh more. It was very painful. All this time the old lady with the smile was watching us.

"If you don't stop laughing," Fish said finally, "I'm going to leave."

I calmed down and poured the tea for everyone. I was back to being grand. We stuffed ourselves with the goodies. I have never seen Lacey eat so much. And Fish managed to keep his mouth shut while he was eating, most of the time. We even had some civilized conversation.

"Do you remember the time we went to the opera?" I asked.

"Oh yes," said Fish. "It was in London, wasn't it, after the war?"

Lacey giggled at everything we said. It is very nice to have someone who thinks everything you say is funny.

"Miss Birdie was there," I said. "Everyone who is anyone was there."

"Everyone but the doctor," Lacey said suddenly. "So when Miss Birdie dropped dead, there was nothing anyone could do."

Fish and I looked at each other in shock. "Lacey!" we both said at the same time. She was bright red. And then the three of us laughed so hard I thought I was going to be sick.

The waitress came over with the check. She was definitely trying to get rid of us. She handed it to me, and I felt very important. But when I looked at it, I didn't feel so great. My heart beat too fast, and my hands turned clammy. I didn't have near enough money. "Do you have any money?" I whispered to Fish and Lacey. They shook their heads. I dug into the pocket of my church coat, thinking I would find more change there. I bit my lip, trying to think of what to do. Didn't people offer to wash dishes in cases like this? Or maybe I could ask them to charge it to me?

Fish said, "It's really late, Lydia. We ought to be getting back for dinner."

Lacey said, "We're going to get in so much trouble."

I wanted to kill them both. They were worried about getting into trouble at Pocket when this was real trouble. I held the check with trembling fingers. The sniffly waitress was beginning to look sour.

And then the old lady with the smile was standing beside me. "I would like to take care of that," she said. She took the bill right out of my hand. "Watching you has given me so much pleasure, I insist on making your morning's outing my treat." She reached down and grasped my trembling hand. "Mrs. Walker," she said.

"Lydia Rice," I said. "But I can't let you pay," I said, suddenly coming to my senses. What was I thinking of?

"So nice to meet you, Lydia, and of course you can.

You and your pals remind me so much of my own school gang."

"Speaking of school, we have to get back," said Fish.

"But this is Sunday," said Mrs. Walker.

"Sunday dinner," said Fish. "At Pocket boarding school."

"I went to Pocket," said Mrs. Walker. "What a wonderful coincidence."

"You went to Pocket?" I almost leaped into the air, and my words came out in a rush. "Do you know about the mural? The mural at the bottom of the stairs?"

She said, "Yes, of course. I'm in the mural."

At this important moment, Fish said, "We'll be outside. Hurry up."

I shouted, "You're not Elizabeth Longford, but you could be Dottie, Bunny, Abby, or Connie!"

"Goodness!" Mrs. Walker exclaimed.

"We're going to leave without you," said Fish. He turned and stormed out of the Tea Shoppe, slamming the door behind him.

"How in the world do you know all this?" Mrs. Walker asked. "I am Abby."

"Abby Webb," I said, completely pleased with myself. "You are sitting with a white kitten."

"Biscuit," said Mrs. Walker. "She was as white as a powder biscuit. I loved that cat. It belonged to Mr. Pendragon, the art teacher."

"You wrote a play called 'The Pink Egg'!"

Mrs. Walker just about died. "How on earth?"

Fish came banging back into the shoppe. "Come on, Lydia, we have to go!"

Mrs. Walker said, "You'd better go, Lydia, but you must come and visit me. I live just down the street, you know, in the yellow house on the corner of Chestnut and Elm. You can come and tell me everything!"

"One last thing," I said as I headed toward the door. "Can you tell me what the letters in the border mean? The A–B–C–D–E and the WHEEL?"

Mrs. Walker smiled at me. "Ah," she said with her beautiful smile. "A smart girl like you can easily figure that out."

"That's what Elizabeth Longford said."

"Lizzy!" Mrs. Walker exclaimed again.

"We're leaving," said Fish, pulling me by the arm.

"Thank you, Mrs. Walker, for everything!" I said, going out the door.

"You are more than welcome, my dear. You simply made my day!"

"Mine, too," I called.

And then we were out the door. There was this incredible snowstorm going on, and we hadn't even noticed it. Lacey and I only had our flimsy church shoes on. We slipped on the new snow and at first didn't even know how to get back to school. But Fish recognized where we were, so we ran and slid on purpose. We threw snowballs at each other (even Lacey did) until our stupid white gloves got sopping wet and our hands were freezing. We made it back in time for supper, and *no* one knew we had been gone all that time in the secret and magical Tea Shoppe. Where Mrs. Walker saved me from shameful debt.

As soon as I could, I ran down to the mural and looked at Abby Wells. I patted the kitten and said, "Hi Biscuit." Then I rubbed Lizzy's nose and wished for a snow day.

I am looking out the window right now, making sure it is still snowing. It is snowing like hippos and elephants. I bet we do have a snow day tomorrow.

Monday, February 8

We have a snow day today.

As soon as breakfast was over, I went to find Howie. He was outside, shoveling snow. He'd shovel a bit and then stop, shovel a bit and then stop. His eyes were watery, and his nose was red and veiny. I thought maybe he was too old to be shoveling snow. How come the Pocket School didn't hire a younger man?

"I'll help shovel," I said.

"I'm almost done here," he said.

"I used to shovel for Gran all the time," I said. "It's fun."

"Fun for about five minutes," he said.

"Howie, I found Abby!"

"What?"

"Abby Webb. In the mural. She's Mrs. Walker now."

Howie leaned on the shovel and smiled a big smile. "Well, isn't that something! How'd you manage to do that?"

I started to tell him, and then I remembered we probably shouldn't have gone into the Tea Shoppe. I didn't know if Howie would tell on me or not. "We ran into her coming back from church. She was really friendly and liked how Fish, Lacey, and I were laughing. She said we reminded her of her old gang at the Pocket School, and we said we went to the Pocket School. Of course I asked about the mural. She said she was in the mural! She said we could come over to her house. She lives right by here."

"Does she now?" Howie asked.

His tone of voice made me suspicious. "You knew that all along," I said. Howie didn't say anything. He just stood there, his face not showing any expression.

"By the way, Howie, have you turned anything into anyone lately? I mean, you're a Silly Wizard and all."

He narrowed his eyes at me. "You know Nellie, our cook, don't you?"

"Of course."

"Well, not that long ago, she was a cute little wire-haired terrier. Her owners weren't very nice. She asked me what I could do about it."

I burst out laughing. "Oh Howie," I said. "Stop it!"

"You're going to accomplish this task, Lydia," he said. "You're two-fifths of the way there."

Then I came inside.

Now I am sitting on my bed and actually writing in the daytime. No flashlight under the covers. I cleaned up my side of the room. I mean really cleaned it, the drawers and closet and everything. There were silverfish at the bottom of my closet under the dirty clothes. I usually don't mind bugs, but this was *disgusting*. I don't think I want to be an entomologist.

I made my bed, I mean really made it, not just pulling up the covers quickly for inspection. I wonder if Mrs. Prokopovich was a silverfish before she was a house-mother. I mean she kind of scuttles around, hides behind things, and pops out when you least expect her to.

Mrs. Fisk just came in and said she would help me with any work I was having trouble with. So I am going to go.

Later . . .

I just got back from working on math in Mrs. Fisk's office. She also helped me with some English grammar. I don't understand how I can like writing so much when I am so bad at grammar.

All my homework is done now, and I like that feeling. I'm going to write a long letter to Mom. Then I'm going to write to Elizabeth Longford and tell her I met Abby. And then I'm going to start reading *Jane Eyre*. I haven't been able to read for a long time. We never have time to read at boarding school.

Later . . .

I have to admit, Pocket isn't as bad as the boarding school Jane Eyre went to. I feel like I am like Jane Eyre, and Lacey is good like Helen Burns.

Right now Lacey is on her bed, writing a letter. It is nicer with Lacey these days. She still is pretty quiet, but now I don't feel she is quiet because she doesn't like me. I know she is quiet because she just is.

With all the snow going on outside, Pocket House feels like a ship going through a storm at sea.

Later again . . .

I went to lunch, which I was dreading, because we have new tables. I am at Mr. O'Rabbit's, and Collie is there, too. That's bad luck, to go from Whitney to Collie. But Mr. O'Hare wasn't at lunch. A lot of the teachers weren't at lunch. Only Mrs. P. and Mrs. Fisk. A lot of the girls weren't in the dining room because a bunch of them were caught smoking. They are in big trouble.

The whole dining room felt different with fewer people and more exciting, I guess, because of the snow day and the trouble, and also because no one was really in charge. We had "make your own sandwiches." I decided it was time to try to be a lead dog even if Collie was sitting there looking superior. (I just realized Collie is a dog's name, ha-ha.)

The dining room tables are round. I suggested we put different sandwich stuff on our plates, like turkey on one, roast beef on another, lettuce on another, pickles on another, bread on another, and then lift the table from underneath and turn it so we'd get a new plate. Then we could take more stuff and turn the table again and so on. Everyone looked at me as if I was crazy. But then Liz Atkinson, who is a senior, burst out laughing and said we should try it. So we all, Collie included, put our hands underneath the table. We turned it one place setting at a time. It was completely funny and fun. Even Collie laughed.

Later again . . .

Mrs. Fisk said Fish, Lacey, and I could go sledding. Lacey wasn't sure she wanted to go out in the cold, but I let her borrow some of my warm Minnesota winter stuff. She pulled a blue scarf out of her drawer. She held it in her hands for a moment. "It was my mother's," she said. She wrapped it around her neck.

When we got outside, it had stopped snowing. Everything was sparkling and dazzling in the sun. Lacey just stood there in her blue scarf and stared. Then she said in her soft southern accent, "It's so beautiful!" Fish came rushing toward us with three sleds. He was wearing this furry cap with furry flappy ears and looked really funny.

"Nice hat," said Lacey.

He said, "It's my father's old hat. Like it? He got it in Russia!"

I think Mom would have said it was poetic that Lacey was wearing her mom's scarf and Fish was wearing his dad's hat.

We pulled the sleds down the middle of the street. Nothing had been plowed. All the cars were buried under snow on either side of us. They were white and lumpy. I pretended they were dinosaurs. It was quiet, like the woods. With my head down, I could even imagine I was at Hidden Lake.

On the hill, it took us a while to pack down the snow so it was good for sledding, but finally it was perfect. We went up and down a million times, and then raced and crashed into each other. After that Fish and I tried coming down standing up on the sleds. We lasted about two seconds. Lacey refused to try.

Other kids started coming, kids we didn't know. I liked that because it made me feel as if we were regular kids, not boarding school kids, and that after sledding we would go home to real houses. I wondered why no other girls from Pocket were sledding. Fish said it was because girls reach a certain age and don't want to do anything but sit around. Maybe he is right, but I am *never* going to be like that.

Suddenly as I came down from a run, I realized we

were on the corner of Chestnut Street and Elm. There was a yellow house, which is where Mrs. Walker lives. So when Lacey and Fish came down, I said, "Let's go visit Mrs. Walker."

They asked, "Who?"

I said, "The old lady with the smile in the Tea Shoppe. The one who paid for us."

They asked, "Why?"

I said, "Because I am lead dog. If you don't want to come, I am going to go without you." I marched off, pulling my sled, and sure enough the two of them followed like puppies.

Mrs. Walker's house has a porch with stairs so I went up and rang her doorbell. My heart was pounding a bit because it seemed nervy all of a sudden to be doing this. A few seconds later, Mrs. Walker and three dogs came to the door. When she saw me, her whole face lit up with her beautiful smile.

"Lydia Rice!" she said. "Would you like to come in?" I nodded. Then she saw Lacey and Fish, and said, "And you've brought your friends. Come in and take your things off in the hall."

The whole time she was talking, the dogs were pushing around her, tails wagging. She kept saying, "Max [black with shiny, slippery short hair], behave yourself"; "Sidney [yellow, or golden, I guess, with longish hair], you just hold on a minute"; "Baxter [white and black, big, and very shaggy], where are your manners?"

She was wearing a skirt, a flowered blouse, and a sweater that didn't quite fit because of her, well, plumpness. Her hair was still pinned back with bobby pins. She was just as nice-looking to me as she had been in the Tea Shoppe.

As we came in, the dogs lunged, wagging, licking, and drooling, pressing their bodies against us. It felt like being in the ocean and being swept up by waves. Mrs. Walker kept yelling, "Max, Sidney, Baxter, behave yourselves."

When we finally had our outside clothes off, she and the dogs pushed us into the living room. The fattest and oldest dog (brown and white, a sort of spaniel, I think, with *really* cute curly hair and floppy ears) was lying on a couch. Her tail twitched when we walked in. Mrs. Walker said, "Mollie is the queen around here." Opposite on another couch were two fat cats, one black and the other one white. "I don't know where anyone is supposed to sit," Mrs. Walker complained. She bustled around, shoving the cats off one couch and heaving Mollie off the other couch. Mollie was so fat and old she wobbled when she hit the floor. With a big groan, she collapsed in a heap. "So sorry, your majesty," Mrs. Walker said, "but we have visitors today." She beamed at us and told us to sit down while she went into the kitchen and found some goodies.

The couches were covered with hair. Lacey started sneezing as soon as she sat down. I sat and looked around. There was a fireplace and paintings of birds on the walls. There were old chairs that reminded me of some of the chairs at Hidden Lake and shelves stuffed with books. There was a coffee table covered with garden, house, and antique-furniture magazines. There were two bird cages over by one of the windows, two canaries singing away in one, and pretty green-and-yellow parakeets in the other.

Suddenly the most horrible smell I have ever smelled filled the room. Fish, Lacey, and I looked at each other. Fish asked, "Okay, who did it?" Mrs. Walker came in with a tray of cookies and a pitcher, and said, "Oh, Mollie, you haven't! What a fotty old dog you are. That's what my husband always calls her, fotty old dog. Come on, Mollie, we're banishing you to the kitchen."

She put the tray down on a table between the two couches and leaned down and scooped Mollie into her arms. How she ever did that, I don't know. She must be really strong. While she was gone, Max, Sidney, and Baxter went over to the tray and snuffled, snarfed, and gobbled so by the time she came back, there were nothing but crumbs everywhere. "Oh, you naughty dogs," she said and then looked at us. "You should have stopped them!" she scolded.

"But it happened so fast," I said. Mrs. Walker laughed

and said, "Never mind. There's more where those came from," and she swung back out of the living room.

Max and Sidney climbed up on the couch where Lacey was sitting by herself. She squealed, "Oooh," curled up as small as she could get, sneezed some more while the two dogs nudged each other for the best spot. They finally settled down with their heads on Lacey's knees, drooling ever so slightly, while she sat so still she looked frozen, except when she sneezed. Baxter lunged up on the other couch between Fish and me. That dog had the worst bad breath of any dog I have ever met. Mrs. Walker came back in with more cookies, and I guess she didn't see Mollie waddling sneakily in behind her.

"Well!" she said, looking over the whole scene. "I see everybody has made themselves at home here." Lacey sneezed again, and Mrs. Walker said, "Oh, poor dear, you must be allergic." She hauled Max and Sidney off Lacey, and Baxter off us.

"There!" she said finally as she plopped herself down beside Lacey. As soon as she did that, Mollie kind of pulled herself over to the couch, belly to the floor, maybe trying to act as if she were small and invisible or something, and groaned as she rested her head on Mrs. Walker's feet.

"Now help yourself to cookies and lemonade," Mrs. Walker said. "Lydia, I want you tell me how you know so much about the mural."

I shook my head and made a face at her. "Can't talk about that right now," I said. The last thing I wanted was Fish deciding he was going to help with the Silly Wizard task.

"What mural?" asked Fish. My heart sank. Unfortunately Fish is like this leech that hooks onto something and doesn't let go. "The mural at school? What about the mural?"

I made another face, and Mrs. Walker said, "What I really want to hear about is what Pocket life is like right now. Lydia and I can talk later."

Pretty soon Fish and I were telling funny stories about school. We did imitations of everyone from Mr. O'Hare to Miss Birdie to Miss Sparring. Mrs. Walker laughed so hard she was crying. Lacey didn't say a word, but in between sneezes she laughed almost harder than Mrs. Walker. Every now and then Mrs. Walker would get up (all the dogs would get up too except for Mollie, who would sort of stretch, groan, and look puzzled) and go out to the kitchen and bring back more cookies and lemonade.

Fish was just telling her about the pig heart in Mr. O'Hare's closet when all of a sudden the dogs jumped up. We heard the front hall door open, and Mrs. Walker said, "Oh, Lionel's home."

Lacey suddenly screamed, "It's dark outside! It's so late!" Fish, Lacey, and I looked at each other in a panic.

Mrs. Walker said, "Oh my, they'll be frantic at the

school. Lionel," she called, "we need you! Come on in, darling, right away. We need you to call Pocket School." She put an arm around Lacey and said, "Now don't you worry one bit, Lacey." As usual I was jealous. I wished I could be delicate like Lacey so Mrs. Walker would comfort me.

The dogs rushed back in, whimpering, whining, and wagging their tails as a large, tall man with white hair sticking up every which way came into the room. He reminded me somehow of one of those old sailing ships, with tall masts and billowing sails. He said, "Well, well, I see we have visitors."

Mrs. Walker said, "Lionel, you've got to call Archie right away and tell him we have some of his kids and that they've been with me and mustn't get into trouble. Then you must run them right back to school. Lydia, Lacey, and Fish, this is my husband, Dr. Walker."

We all raised our eyebrows at each other because Archie had to be our headmaster, Mr. Wing.

"Runaways, eh?" said Dr. Walker, still smiling.

"No!" said Lacey, frightened, and Dr. Walker said, "Just fooling, my dear."

"Get your boots and jackets on, dears, while Dr. Walker is calling. Then he'll be able to whisk you back." So we rose up sadly from the hairy couches. As we were struggling to put on our wet, soggy stuff, Mrs. Walker said, "Lydia, we must arrange a time to talk."

We heard Dr. Walker's voice as he shouted into the phone. "Archie? Is that you? This is Lionel Walker. We've got three of your children here, two beautiful lasses and a comely lad. Yes, yes, Lacey, Lydia, and Fish. Are you Alexander?" he shouted at us, and Fish shouted back, "Yes." "Yes, yes, invited in by Abigail, yes, yes, should have let the school know. Been looking for them everywhere, have you? Well, you know how Ab can be. Time goes by, and she doesn't realize it. Not the children's fault. Now, Archie, we won't have that. They're safe and sound, that's the important thing. I'll run them right over."

"Can you tell me anything more about Dottie and Connie?" I asked in a rush, because I had to find out.

"Connie," Mrs. Walker said, "is a photographer. And Dottie and Pen got married, we all knew they would some day."

"Dottie and who?" I asked.

"Dottie and Mr. Pendragon, our heavenly art teacher, the one who painted the mural."

"Mr. *Pendragon* painted the mural?"

"Yes, of course."

"I thought Miss Pocket painted it. P for Pocket."

"P for Pendragon," said Mrs. Walker with a smile.

Dr. Walker said, "Bus is leaving."

First there was a commotion with the dogs again as

we went out the door; and then *bam*, we stepped from the warm, cozy house into the cold night.

The street was scraped clean. A lot of the cars had been dug out. They didn't look like dinosaurs anymore.

As long as I was in the car, there was still a doggy, musty smell. Dr. Walker's big, heavy, winter coat made me feel safe as I sat beside him in the front seat. It reminded me of when I was little, and Mom, Dad, and I would drive home from Hidden Lake in the wintertime at night. I'd crawl under blankets in the backseat of the car, and it would feel as if I were in a moving nest.

It's funny I was thinking that because all of a sudden Fish leaned forward from the backseat and said, "You know how, when it's snowing at night and you are driving and turn the headlights on, you see the snow coming down?" Everyone said yes. He said, "And when you turn the headlights off, the snow disappears?" Everyone said yes. He said, "Well, when I was a little kid, I thought that when my father turned the headlights on, he made the snow."

That made me realize that Fish probably still misses his father. Maybe we realized it because, for the rest of the way back to school, we were all quiet.

As soon as we stepped into Pocket House, we were back in stale, dusty air and old-lady perfume. The lights were too bright, and there was a fuss all around us, from

Mrs. Fisk, Mr. O'Hare, Miss Hammer, Miss Sparring, and Mr. Wing. They weren't mean while Dr. Walker and Mr. Wing were there, but as soon as those two left, they circled us like a pack of wolves and told us how thoughtless and irresponsible we were.

I glanced at Lacey, and she crossed her eyes at me ever so slightly. I thought for a moment I was going to giggle. In that moment I realized something about Lacey. She's not as good as she seems.

When we were finally allowed to go upstairs, our room filled up with girls—Liz Atkinson, Collie, and a bunch of others. "Where were you?" they wanted to know. "Did you run away?" They sat on our beds and told us all about the girls who had gotten into trouble for smoking. And guess what? Whitney was one of them. Whitney has been suspended! Collie said, "I'm so glad I wasn't with her. My parents would have killed me."

During quiet-hour Lacey said, "My father is coming next Thursday. I'm going to stay with him in a hotel over the long weekend. Do you want to go out to dinner with us on Thursday night?" I said, "Sure." She said, "Good, I want you to meet him." I thought, Wow, we are friends now.

Tuesday, February 9

Today in history class I was looking through the text-book, just leafing through it because Mr. O'Hare was being especially boring. When I got to the section on World War II, there was a picture of a bombed-out village. A woman was standing in the picture with her child. Underneath the picture in small letters, it said CONSTANCE EISLER. I yelled, "Ahh!" or something like that.

Mr. O'Hare stopped talking, and came and stood over me. He asked, "Whatever is the matter?"

I pointed to the picture and said, "She went to Pocket. Connie Eisler, who took that photograph, went to Pocket."

Mr. O'Hare stood there with his glasses pushed down on the end of his nose. He said, "Lydia, take your books and go out into the hall. You may not be in this class until you are ready to give it your full attention."

So I have to go for Saturday detention. I would have thought he'd be excited about Connie Eisler.

Mrs. Fisk helped me with my homework again. Why does she like that stupid Mr. O'Hare? I don't get it.

I found Howie after school. He was actually coming out of his door so I grabbed him by the arm and pulled him over to the mural.

"I know who painted this," I said. "Someone whose name begins with P."

"Florence Pocket," he said.

"Nope," I said, gleeful. "Mr. Pendragon."

Howie's tangly eyebrows went right up. "Mr. Pendragon?"

"He ended up marrying Dottie." Howie didn't say anything. "That's what Abby told me."

"Abby!" he exclaimed.

So I told him all about yesterday.

"Well," he said, when I had finished. "Going to her house! It was meant to happen!"

"Do you *know* Mrs. Walker?" I asked.

"I know *all* creatures. I am a Silly Wizard."

"Yeah, sure, but Mrs. Walker isn't a creature. She's a person, and you said yourself you've been around here for a long time, so you must know her."

"I know the Abby on the mural," he said.

"I don't get what that means."

"It means I know the Abby on the mural."

"I am beginning to figure out who is who," I told him. "That's Abby with the kitten. The paint's faded so it isn't that easy to tell. Dottie must be the one reading because she was the serious, quiet one. Connie is painting, and I think Bunny is in the tree." I looked at the border again. "A–B–C–D–E and WHEEL," I said, tracing the letters with a finger. "I still have no idea what that means."

I hopped back from the painting and ran up the stairs until I came to the middle one and sat down.

Howie came up the stairs and sat beside me. His pants were covered with blobs of paint. I could see the cuffs at the bottom were frayed. So were the cuffs of his shirt for that matter. Sometimes Howie seems magical to me, and sometimes he seems—well, sometimes I worry about him.

"Tell me about your life," I said.

"My life?" He turned to look at me. "Really, Lydia, you don't ask for much, do you."

"You were married, right? Did you have kids? Where do you live and stuff?" I suddenly wanted to know, and it was making me mad he never told me anything.

"Kind of nosey, ain't ya?" he said, gruffly.

"Well?" I wasn't going to let him off the hook.

"Well, Lydia, what can I tell you? I was married, as you know. We never had children, but we did have all sorts of young friends."

"What did you do? Were you always working here? I mean fixing things and being the night watchman?"

Howie smiled and shook his head. He sighed and pulled on his beard. "My wife and I worked in schools together, teaching, painting, writing."

"You *were* an art teacher!" I yelled.

"Hello, excuse me." Mr. O'Hare was at the bottom of the stairs, looking up at us. We were blocking his way.

"Sorry, we're just moving," said Howie, standing up.

"Shouldn't you be getting ready for dinner?" Mr. O'Hare asked me as he walked passed us.

"I've got time," I said.

"Don't be late," he said in his bossiest I'm-in-charge voice.

"How about more of the story?" I asked as soon as Mr. O'Hare was gone.

"You'd better go, Lydia," Howie said.

I jumped back down and rubbed the jump-rope girl's nose. Elizabeth's nose. Lizzy's nose.

"What'd you wish?" he asked.

"If you tell, wishes don't come true," I said. I ran up the stairs without even saying *rach manji*.

What I wished was that Howie's stories would get published. Maybe that's a crazy wish, but it's what popped into my head as I was standing there.

Wednesday, February 10

Wow! I got another letter from Elizabeth Longford today! She said she is glad I met Abby. She said, "Abby Webb has a genius for friendship." And she said I am inspiring her to think about visiting because she hasn't been back to Pocket in ages. She is seeing if she can find out where the others are and get them to come, too.

There was a trustee meeting today at school. I'm not sure what a trustee is, someone who is important, I guess, because Miss Sparring and Mr. O'Hare made us clean everything up more than usual. There was a fancy dinner here tonight for them, after we ate our gruel, cold porridge, and stale bread. Some of the older girls were waitresses.

Before that, though, this afternoon, all the trustees had a meeting in the big sitting room. Their winter coats and hats were piled on the chests in the hallway during the meeting. Lacey, Fish, and I were hanging around in the hallway before supper when Fish suddenly grabbed one of the men's hats, punched his fist into it, and popped the crease out of it.

"Why'd you do that?" I asked.

"Because," he said. "I don't like these stupid hats." He was about to pick up another one and do the same thing when the doors to the sitting room opened. People started coming out, men in suits and women all dressed up, talking and laughing. Mr. Wing and Dr. Walker came out.

"Oh, hello," said Dr. Walker, looking at us. "How nice to see you. Abby was just saying we should have you over to the house again."

He picked up his hat, which turned out to be the one Fish had punched. He turned it around in his hands and stared at it with a frown between his eyes. Then he looked straight at me and again at his hat. I looked around for Fish, but he was gone. More people came out, including Mr. O'Hare and Miss Sparring, who, for them, were more dressed up than usual. Miss Sparring was wearing lipstick!

"I didn't do that," I said quickly to Dr. Walker, pointing to his hat. "No harm done," he said, putting the crease back into it. I was sure he didn't believe me. "We'll see you soon, I hope, Lydia," he said, but I didn't believe him. I thought he was disgusted with me. I ran off because my face was burning, and there were worms in my stomach.

I can't go to the Walkers anymore. I can't ask Abby—

Mrs. Walker—anything more about the mural because she won't want me in their house. I want to punch Fish right in his gut just the way he punched that hat.

I am thinking about how at supper we had apples for dessert. I twisted the stem and said the alphabet, and it came out on F. F for Fish. Ugh. Then I tried paring it and the peel broke right at the beginning. Which just shows how unlucky I am.

Lacey's father is coming up from Georgia. He is coming next Thursday so he can meet Lacey's teachers and talk to them. That night I am going out to dinner with them. I am still mad at Fish for making Dr. Walker think I punched his hat in. Fish is such a brat. I hope his mother *does* marry Mr. O'Hare and that they all live together and that Mr. O'Hare makes life a torment for Fish.

I am making up an alphabet code.

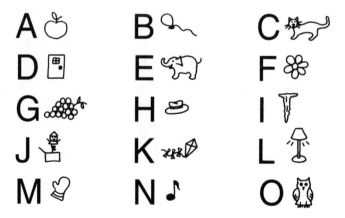

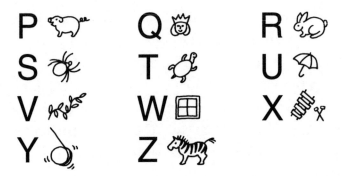

Collie just came into our room and asked me what I was doing. I said, "Nothing." She said, "No, what is it?" I said, "You'll think it's dumb." She said, "Let me see."

I showed her the alphabet and she said, "That's neat. Maybe Lacey and I can copy it, and we can write messages to each other."

I let her have the alphabet, and now she and Lacey are sitting on Lacey's bed, copying it. Collie spends a lot of time here now that Whitney's away. She said that Whitney got into so much trouble with her parents she might not be allowed to come back to Pocket.

I don't want to go to Dad-and-April's for the long weekend. I want to go to Mom's, but it is too far.

In the middle of copying the alphabet, Collie got to the P, which is the pig with the curly tail, and she laughed and said, "Do you think it's true Mr. O'Hare has a pig heart in his closet?"

"I wish we could find out for sure," said Lacey.

While Collie and Lacey are sitting here working on the alphabet, I am picturing all those keys hanging in the maintenance room. I think I am getting a brilliant idea.

I just glanced over at their alphabets to see how they're doing. Lacey is only on the H. She is slow and careful about everything she does. Collie is almost finished. She is terrible at drawing. Oh well. At least she is being fun and acting like a kid.

Thursday, February 11

Today I said to Collie and Lacey, "Let's leave messages for each other in the hole in the bottom of the maple tree."

Here is the message I left for Lacey and Collie.

Later . . .

I found three messages in the tree.

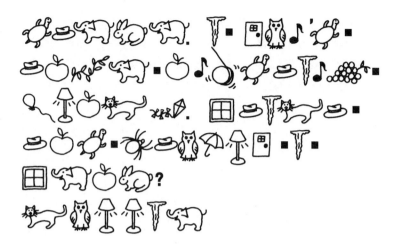

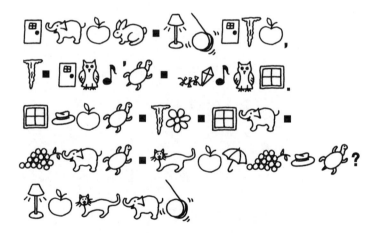

The third one was from Fish, not in code. Can you believe the nerve of the boy?

Dear Lydia,

You ought to invent a harder code. This one is

too easy to crack. How come you left me out of Operation Pig Heart? How are you going to do it? And also, Howie goes around the school at night, you know. And also, if you don't include me, I'll tell my mother.

Sincerely yours,

I wrote back to Lacey and Collie.

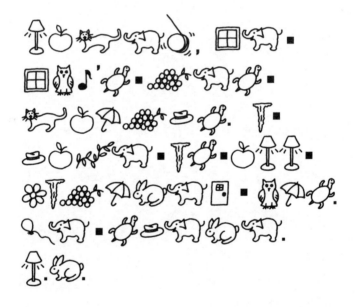

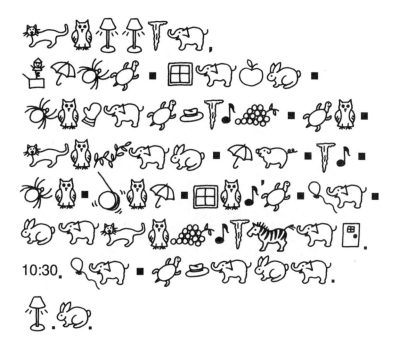

And then I left Fish a note, too.

I know all about Howie and when his rounds are. I will let you in only if you call Dr. Walker and tell him you are the one who punched his hat. He thinks I did it. You think of a better code if you don't like ours.

Not sincerely yours,
L. R.

Later . . .

Fish actually called Mrs. Walker and told her he was the one who punched in the hat. I guess she just laughed, and Dr. Walker hadn't even mentioned it. Fish said I made a big fuss over nothing.

This afternoon Howie and I worked on the water clock. It's still hard to get the water to drip slowly.

Howie said, "It's like time itself. It's hard to control. It either rushes by, or drags."

"Like when you're in math class," I said. "Or almost any class. Why is school so boring, Howie? I wish I could make time go fast when I'm in school and slow when I'm on vacation. Except when I'm at Dad-and-April's. And I have to go there on the long weekend."

"Dad-and-April's?" Howie asked.

I ended up telling him about Mom and Dad. I didn't mean to. It all just came out, like the water gushing too fast out of the orange juice cans when I first tried to make the clock. And blistering bleeding crustaceans, I started to cry. I kept wiping my face with the back of my sleeve. I was worried some stupid girls would come by and see me crying—or even worse, Fish.

After I had finished, Howie said, "It's probably hard for you to understand, Lydia, but in the end, all this will make you a better Silly Wizard."

"That doesn't make sense."

"It does, but I don't expect you to believe me; however, you might have a better time at your Dad's if you try to believe me. Now we are going to need a handful of tiny screws, a tiny screwdriver, and something like a bicycle chain."

I followed Howie out of the lunchroom to the maintenance room. I saw the school keys hanging on the wall. Here was my golden opportunity.

I cleared my throat and tried to sound casual. "Howie, did you tell me that the same key that opens the classrooms also opens the closets in the classrooms?"

"Yup," he said, his head down as he opened and shut drawers, looking for tools.

"How about to the classroom buildings—like Duckworth—is that a separate key?"

"All one key. Makes it easier for the teachers. One key opens everything."

Can I borrow the Duckworth key so we can look into Mr. O'Hare's closet? The words were just sitting there on the tip of my tongue.

How dumb could I be? Of course he'd say no.

I thought about taking the keys while he was rummaging around. I could just *borrow* them. I'd be really careful not to lose them or anything. Although I don't know. It would be like stealing.

Friday, February 12

I left a message for Lacey, Collie, and Fish in the tree at recess. I wrote:

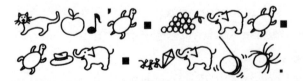

In history class, Collie passed me a note. It said:

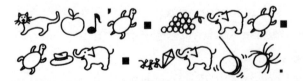

I wrote back:

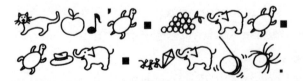

Collie passed my note to Fish. He read it and frowned. Well, I thought Lacey wouldn't mind because she's scared to do it anyway. But she read the note and gave me the oddest look, as if I had let her down in a big way.

After supper tonight Lacey went up to Collie's room. She's never done that before. I am sitting on my bed alone in my room and writing this.

I think it's really dumb if they are all mad at me.

I thought I might tell Howie about Operation Pig Heart after school and how the others are being mean. When I knocked on his door, he came out looking terrible. His eyes were red, and he looked as if he hadn't slept in a long time. I said I wouldn't stay.

"No, no, Lydia, you cheer me up," he said. "To tell the truth, I've been having one of my bad spells. Do you want to work on the water clock?"

"To tell the truth, I don't really feel like it," I said. All I wanted to do was ask him about the keys.

"Well, maybe another time," said Howie. "Must be that dance class is wearing you out."

I said, "Yeah." Then I sat down on the stairs. I didn't feel like going back to my room.

I sat on the stairs and stared at the mural. I pretended that I was in the painting, playing with Lizzy, Abby, and the others. All the girls and teachers had to walk around me, but I didn't care. Collie, Fish, and Lacey came down the stairs together.

Collie asked, "Why are you sitting on the stairs?"

"Because I want to," I said.

Fish said, "She's doing it to get attention," and they kept walking.

Inside myself I climbed up that tree in the mural and sat right up there with Bunny.

When I went back up to my room, there was a message for me from Mrs. Walker. She wants me to come over to her house on Saturday. She and Howie are the only friends I have.

Saturday, February 13

After detention, I went over to Mrs. Walker's.

She told me more about Pocket when she was a girl. They had literature, mathematics, Latin, and world history in the morning. They had art, which they called studio, all afternoon.

She told me more about the girls. Connie was the most ambitious one. She went on to make a name for herself. "I was never very ambitious myself," Mrs. Walker said. "I don't know why I ended up in that group of girls. They were all so clever. I think it was because Lizzy was my roommate, and they tolerated me because of her."

"Elizabeth Longford said you had a genius for friendship," I said.

Mrs. Walker turned bright red. "What a nice thing to say!"

She talked about Dottie Ehrenhaft and how sometimes they were jealous of her because she was so pretty. I said I was jealous of Lacey. Mrs. Walker looked at me and said, "Lacey is pretty, but you have character."

I said, "I'd rather be pretty. I don't want to be a character."

"I didn't say you *are* a character. I said you *have* character. Right now your friend Lacey is made of air. She won't always be that way, of course, but you're already more grown-up than she is."

"*Me?*" I squealed. I couldn't believe what she was saying.

Mrs. Walker was smiling her beautiful smile. "Remember I told you I had something special to tell you?"

I nodded.

"Well, you've been reminding me a lot of someone I used to know. I've been wracking my brains. Someone who was a little imp and full of beans, but behind all that was a kind of strength and wisdom. And I got to thinking of my old friend Bunny."

"Bunny? You think I'm like Bunny?" Secretly Bunny was my favorite Pocket girl.

"I got to thinking about your name, Lydia Rice, and it just hit me like a ton of bricks. Lydia! Why didn't you tell me your grandmother went to Pocket?"

I couldn't take in what she was saying. My grandmother? What did she have to do with anything?

Mrs. Walker picked up a photograph that was on one of her bookcases. She handed it to me. It was of a wedding, the bride and groom in the middle, with people on either side of them.

"Anyone you recognize?" she asked.

"Hey, that's Gran in the wedding dress!" I said. "And that must be Grandpa. I never met him. He died before I was born."

"John Rice was a very nice man."

"But how do you—" and then I saw one of the girls in a bridesmaid's dress. She was a bit plump, with a laughing face lit up with a beautiful smile. "You were at my grandmother's wedding!"

"I wouldn't have missed Bunny's wedding for anything," said Mrs. Walker.

"Bunny!" I yelled. "Bunny was my *grandmother!*"

"I was so sad to hear of her death," said Mrs. Walker. "We had talked so often of getting together. The time just slipped by, and the next thing I knew . . . " She sighed and took the photograph from me, looking at it for a moment. "You are so like her! I can't imagine why I didn't spot the resemblance right away, but of course I wasn't thinking about it."

Now I am sitting on my bed, and there is a volcano

inside of me. On the one hand, I am happy that Bunny is my grandmother. On the other hand, when I came back from Mrs. Walker's, I found out Collie and Lacey were over at Fish's. I know Fish invited them on purpose just to be mean to me.

I can't stand it anymore. The way they are treating me.

Tonight I'm going to do something I haven't done in a long time. I am going prowling.

Later . . .

I just got back.

I feel squirmy. I don't know. I don't know if I did the right thing. But it'll be over soon and won't matter.

First of all, though, is the good part. I met Howie just as he was going out on his rounds, and I told him that Mrs. Walker told me Bunny was Gran.

He grinned this huge grin.

"How long have you known Bunny was my grandmother?" I asked him.

"Since before you were born," he said, a typical Howie answer.

"You *knew* her!"

"I knew *her*," he said, pointing to the face poking out of the leaves. "But she didn't wander around after lights-out, at least as far as I know she didn't. You better skedaddle."

"I can't wait to write Elizabeth Longford and tell her. All I have left of the task is the A–B–C–D–E WHEEL. No one will tell me what it means. I bet Gran wouldn't tell me either, if she were still alive."

"No," said Howie, shaking his head. "I bet you're right; but I have to go on my rounds, and you have to go back upstairs."

Well, what happened next wasn't planned.

Howie left, and my heart started hammering. There was all this buzzing inside my ears. I counted to ten. Then I opened the door to the Silly Wizard lair and took a Pocket House key (so we can get back in) and a Duckworth key. According to Howie, the Duckworth key should also open Mr. O'Hare's classroom and his closet.

They are *extra*, after all.

Tomorrow is Valentine's Day.

Sunday, February 14,
Valentine's Day

I wrote them each a note.

10:30

Later . . .

Lacey is talking to me again, and Collie and Fish are acting as if they were never mad at me. I was dreading Valentine's Day, but it is turning out better than I thought it would.

Later . . .

Lacey, Collie, and I have been working all afternoon on what we're going to wear for Operation Pig Heart.

We started out by cutting up our stockings and pulling them down over our heads. Our faces were smashed flat. Lacey looked as if she didn't have any nose at all. Collie's eyes were saggy. I don't think I have ever laughed so hard in my life, but we decided not to use them because it's too hard to breathe.

I have two tests coming up. Mrs. Fisk is going to help

me study. This will be a hard few days because I have to study and also because we have to get ready for Operation Pig Heart.

Monday, February 15

We had our science test today. I think I did pretty well. In history Mr. O'Hare started the class by saying, "One person has received an outstanding mark on this test." Everyone looked at Lisa Gray because she always gets the best marks. Mr. O'Hare looked at her, too, and then he said, "And it was not Lisa." Then he handed me my test, saying, "It was Lydia Rice. We find she does have a brain." There was a big fat 98 on the top of my paper. I was proud, but I also felt a little sorry for Lisa. Mr. O'Hare always finds a way to be mean to somebody.

At recess Fish had the idea that we ought to go to the costume closet for disguises. I didn't even know there was a costume closet. Fish took us to the basement of Pocket Hall, and there were rows and rows of costumes. Yikes! What a find. There are hats and swords and canes and robes and millions of dresses. I wanted to stay there forever.

We tried on different things. Finally Collie settled on this big brown monk's robe. Lacey is going to wear a leopard suit. It has ears and a tail, and she looks cute even though it is a little baggy on her. Fish decided on a flowered dress and a floppy yellow hat. He looks so ridiculous I thought we were going to die from laughing again. And, I, Lydia Rice, am wearing an Army jacket with an Army hat because I am the general. I am going to paint on a mustache.

Tuesday, February 16

I passed my math test! 65. Wow! It's a miracle! And the stuff I got wrong was just little piddly stuff. I can do better, I think.

Tonight is the night. Operation Pig Heart. I can't wait!

Later . . .

Well, tonight was the night. What a disaster! I am going to try to write it all down quickly so I don't forget anything.

A little before ten, Lacey and I went into the day students' bathroom to change into our costumes. I painted on my mustache. We waited and waited for Collie, but she didn't come. I went up to her room, and she was in bed!

"What is going on?" I asked. She said she was afraid to come down because she had gone out to go to the bathroom, and Miss Hammer had been right there in the hallway. I said, "Well, she isn't here now, so grab your stuff and hurry up." We ran downstairs and of course now Lacey was quivery from being left on her own. This was a very shaky group I was working with.

We snuck down the stairs and rubbed Lizzy's nose for luck as we went by. I secretly said hi to Gran. I made sure Lacey and Collie were really quiet outside Howie's door. I pushed open the heavy door and out of Pocket House we went.

The courtyard was eerie and shadowy because each building has an outside floodlight attached to it.

The worst part was that there was a freezing rain, and it was unbelievably slippery. Lacey fell right away because she tripped on her tail. A few seconds later I fell, and then Collie. There was a big, cold wet spot on the side of my leg where I had fallen, and it took forever to get to the tree. Fish wasn't there. We stood under the tree waiting for him, getting colder and colder and wetter and wetter.

Finally we saw this figure, trying to make its way across the courtyard from Corner House. For a moment my heart sank. I thought it was a housemother, but then I realized it was Fish in his disguise. He was halfway to the tree when he fell. *Bam!* It was pretty funny. Collie, Lacey, and I were clutching each other, trying not to laugh too loud. By the time Fish finally reached us, he was red in the face, sweating and cussing up a storm.

"How am I supposed to walk in this stupid thing?" he asked, pulling at the dress.

"What time is it?" I asked.

"Ten-fifteen," said Fish, looking at his watch.

"Come on, we're late," I said. "We don't have much time. Howie will be coming out on his rounds."

Fish wanted to know how I knew that, and I said, "I just know."

He asked, "How?"

I said, "Shut up. Let's just go."

We held on to each other so we wouldn't fall. It was hard to walk, and I was getting more and more nervous.

We finally made it to Duckworth. I got the keys out of my pocket. First I put the Pocket House key into the lock by mistake, and when I tried the one that was marked, "Duck," it didn't work either. Fish said, "I bet it's the key to the side door."

It's lucky Fish has grown up at this school. He knows a lot about it. We slipped and slid around to the side and sure enough, the key worked.

We were in such a hurry to get to Mr. O'Hare's classroom that we didn't pay attention to how the door shut. It shut with a *bang.* I thought I was going to have a heart attack. We had to go up a flight of stairs to get to his room. The steps are metal or something. Every step we took sounded loud and echoey. We passed the science lab. Why didn't Mr. O'Hare keep his pig heart in there?

Finally we were in front of Mr. O'Hare's room, D–6. The key turned in the lock. "Do you have the closet key?" Fish asked.

"It's the same key," I said.

"How do you know?" he asked.

"I just do," I said.

"All right, Miss Know-It-All. Tell me how we're going to see once we do open the door."

I looked around. It was pretty dark in the classroom. I, the general, had forgotten to think about a flashlight. I could have kicked myself. "How are we even going to see the pig heart?" he asked.

"Maybe there's a light in the closet," I said.

I stuck the key into the closet door lock. It turned and clicked. I scrabbled my hand around, feeling for a switch on the wall or for a string dangling from a bulb on the ceiling. Nothing. But my eyes were getting used to the dark, and I could see shelves inside the closet. It seemed as if there might be some sort of glass thing in there.

"I think there might be a jar in the way back," I said.

Lacey and Collie starting squealing. "It's there. It's there," they said. I could feel my heart hammering.

"I'm going in," said Fish. "Here, hold this." He handed

me his floppy hat. He took a step into the closet, another step, and another. Then we heard this smashing sound. Fish yelled, "Oh help!" and there was a crunching sound.

"*What happened?*" we asked.

"There's some sort of bone," said Fish.

"*Bone?*" we all yelled.

"It's all splintered, whatever it is," said Fish. "And I don't feel any jar back here, just a picture in a glass frame. I almost broke that, too."

"I'm turning the light on for one tiny second," I said. "Are you ready?" I could only hope and pray Howie wasn't out there somewhere to see a light on the second floor of Duckworth. I went over by the light switch, held my breath, flicked it on, counted to three, and then flicked it off.

Fish backed out of the closet. "I stepped on some kind of big skull," he said. "I can't tell what it is, but it's not good. I definitely crunched it."

"*A skull?*"

"I think it's a human skull," said Fish. Everyone squealed.

Then we heard a bang from down the hallway. Lacey screamed, and Fish slammed the closet door shut. Without even thinking about it, we grabbed onto each other and pulled ourselves out of the room.

"This way," said Fish, and he sprinted down the hall the opposite way we had come. I started to follow, but remembered we'd left the key in the closet door, so I had to turn back. At the closet door my hand was shaking so much I could barely get the key out of the lock. I raced out of the room, shut the classroom door, and ran; I couldn't see the others anymore. There was a door at the end of the hall, the fire exit, I guess, which we never use. I opened it, and there they were, pounding down the stairs. I couldn't *believe* how much noise they were making.

When I caught up to them, Fish said, "We can go out the basement door." He took us down another hall and through another door. There was a nasty smell in the basement, and it was so dark we couldn't see a thing.

"Hug the wall," said Fish. "The door's over here."

Someone's hand found mine. I think it was Lacey's. I promised myself if I ever got back to my room safe and sound, I would never go prowling outside of Pocket House again.

As we came out of Duckworth, it was still drizzling. Fish said, "See you tomorrow." He took off on his hands and knees because it was so slippery.

We had to get all the way over to Pocket House. We got down on our hands and knees, too. Part of the way over, we saw that someone had made a sand path across the courtyard. Someone? Of course it was Howie. That didn't make me feel too good, but at least we could go pretty fast without breaking our necks.

I put the Pocket House key into the lock, and we were

back in. We tiptoed down the hall. I said *shh* so the others would be especially quiet going by Howie's in case he was in there. I showed them how to keep their weight on the edge of the stairs going up so they wouldn't squeak and groan. (Not Lacey and Collie, but the stairs, although Lacey and Collie sure did plenty of squeaking and groaning, too.)

What a night! I am so glad I am in bed.

So that was that. Operation Pig Heart. Instead of finding a pig heart, we found a skull. Creepy. Much, much worse. Why does Mr. O'Hare have a skull in his closet?

Wednesday, February 17

In history today we sat and stared at the closet all through class. The worst part is wondering when Mr. O'Hare is going to open the door and discover his crunched skull. Maybe he never goes in there.

No, the worst part is that my mustache didn't wash off very well, so everyone's been asking me all day why I have a mustache.

No, the worst part is now I have to return Howie's keys without his knowing I took them. I feel *so* guilty.

I wonder if Howie was the noise we heard last night.

Thursday, February 18

I met up with Howie after school today. Maybe I am imagining it, but he didn't seem as friendly as usual. I kept trying to figure out if he knew what we had done.

I told him I wanted to look at his paintings, so he let me go into the maintenance room. I managed to put the keys back. I'm glad I didn't lose them, and they're back on their hooks. They were like these burning, electric, poisonous things in my pocket.

I asked Howie if we could work on the water clock, but he said he was too tired. He did look tired. He had big puffy circles under his eyes. He asked me when I was leaving for the long weekend, and I said tomorrow. He said, "Have a good time and don't be too hard on April."

"Me be hard on April?" I asked.

"Yes, it's probably hard for her to be a stepmother, you know." The way he said it made me feel bad. It was kind of mean, actually. It made me want to go back to my room, so I said, "Well, see you." I didn't say *rach manji* on purpose.

"Well, see you." he said back.

I hate how things are with Howie. I think he knows and he's mad at me. When I get back from the long weekend, I'm going to tell him everything.

Later . . .

Lacey's dad came tonight and took Lacey and me out to dinner. He is the nicest man I've ever met, except for Howie. He is also the tallest man I've ever met. He took us to a really fancy restaurant, and we had lobster. He is funny and easy to talk to. Lacey talked a lot, too. We told him stories about the housemothers. He laughed so much, and what a laugh! He is like the jolly giant. I was jealous of Lacey for having such a nice father, and then I remembered her mom died. But at least she has one parent who comes to visit her and who she can actually talk to. I wish my mother would come visit me. She hardly even writes me, and when she does she sends me poems I don't understand.

Friday, February 19

I am at Dad-and-April's.

Collie, five other girls, and I went to Boston together in a limo they hired just for us. Collie and I sat in the back, and we got talking. I found out she really likes ballet, too. She didn't take dance this winter because she also hates modern dance. I told her my old ballet teacher told me I was too short to be a ballet dancer. She told me her teacher told her she was the wrong body type; in other words she was too fat. We decided that when we are older we are going to start a ballet company and call it the School of Ballet for the Wrong Body Type. Skinny girls will not be allowed, and we will become famous throughout the world. I never would have guessed Collie liked ballet, or that she and I would get along together so well. I was actually sad to get out of the limo. Collie said, "I only live an hour from Boston, so maybe we can get together this weekend. What's your number?" I gave it to her, and the next thing I knew, April was standing there.

April kissed me and acted happy to see me, but I kept thinking it was just an act. She said Dad couldn't come because he had to work late. I wanted to say, "He always has to work late," but I didn't because April freezes all the badness inside of me.

As we were walking to her car, it hit me that April and I have never, ever been alone together. I tried to think of a time when we had been, but I couldn't. I realized she always has a friend over when Dad isn't home. She's afraid to be alone with me. She's afraid of *me*, Lydia. Ha. I thought of what Howie had said. Maybe being a stepmother was hard for her.

I sat beside her in the front seat of the car and stared at her the best I could out of the corners of my eyes. She is *so* different from my mother. She is sharp and bony. Mom is soft and round. Mom reads books and likes folk music. April reads ladies' magazines and goes to the symphony. Mom likes kids. April is afraid of them.

I've decided April is like Emily Barnett at school. Emily has a single room fixed up to look like a real room. She has a nice rug on the floor, a bookcase, an armchair, and a couple of paintings on the walls. She keeps a vase with flowers on her bureau. She always dresses up for supper. She wears makeup, lipstick, and a pearl necklace.

She's in modern dance and loves it. She's the kind of girl April probably was.

If April were my age, she wouldn't bother me at all. Maybe I have to pretend we are the same age.

Oh, blistering barnacles, things weren't so confusing before we moved, before Mom moved. Mom is the one who caused all the problems. If she hadn't moved, we'd still be living in our old house. I wouldn't be in a stupid boarding school, and Dad would never have met April.

What is Mom doing in Minnesota, anyway? Why did she want to move?

I am sitting at my desk in my room at April's house. My desk has little cubbies with paper clips and ink, and it has a clean piece of blotting paper on it and a little china dog. April gave the desk to me for my birthday last year.

Right now I like writing at this desk. I have to admit that when things are neat, my brain feels less tangled up.

Blast blistering crustaceans. April just came in and told me to go to bed. I don't *need* a housemother everywhere I go.

173

Saturday, February 20

I woke up this morning and didn't know where I was. Then I saw lacy curtains. Everything in this room is frilly and lacy. This should be Lacey's room.

April made pancakes for breakfast. At least she is a better cook than Nellie. She uses real maple syrup. When Dad came into the kitchen, he surprised me by giving me a big hug, which he never does. He said, "How'd you like to drive to New Hampshire and see Gran's house?"

My heart zoomed up. I jumped out of my chair and leaped around. Dad laughed and said, "I take it you would like to!"

And guess what? April laughed, too.

Dad said, "You had a nice report from your teachers."

I thought, So that's it. He's only being nice and happy and glad to see me because I'm doing better in school.

"And what's even better, we had a nice letter from Miss Sparring."

"From Miss Sparring?"

"Why don't you let her read it," April suggested.

Dad said, "Good idea." He left the kitchen to go find the letter.

April said, "He was so happy to get this letter. He has been worried about you."

"He *has*?" I said but it came out in a yell. I thought, Uh-oh, the bees are coming out. I'm not going to be able to stop them, and they're going to sting somebody to death.

April pressed her lips together and said. "Yes, he has," in this hard voice, and all the angry bees zipped back down to the bottom of my stomach.

Dad came back and handed me the letter. It was in Miss Sparring's handwriting, which is tall and spiky like her.

Dear Mr. Rice,

I am taking a moment to write you to let you know how pleased we are with Lydia's progress this term. She seems to be taking a greater interest in her studies and in completing her homework assignments. She is also taking more responsibility for her belongings.

She has a fine, lively spirit. It is good to see her begin to use her energy in constructive and positive ways. She has the potential to be a real leader.

With best wishes,
Elva Sparring

Elva? What kind of name is that? Oh well, I never thought Miss Sparring would write a letter like that about me.

I am in my room now, writing quickly. April is packing a lunch for Dad and me. April's not going with us. I'm glad.

Now it's time to go.

Later . . .

We are home, and I have so much to write about.

Dad and I set off for New Hampshire. I didn't know how it would be, just us. I didn't know if he would talk or just have the radio on with classical music playing the whole way. But as soon as we got out of the traffic, he put a hand on my knee, squeezed it, and said, "Well, Lyddie, we're off." Lyddie was the name he used to call me.

"I hope the house is all right. Mr. Turkell is supposed to be keeping an eye on it. I hope he is. Want to know why we're going up?"

I nodded yes. He told me he had auditioned for the symphony orchestra, and they want him! Pretty soon he's going to take a vacation, live at Gran's, and do nothing but concentrate on the viola for two weeks. He said it's all April's idea, she's been encouraging him, and finally he decided to do it. He put his hand on my knee again. "She's a great woman, Lyddie."

I nodded. I didn't think I should tell him she makes me feel frozen.

"She takes care of me," he said. "I know that probably sounds pretty pathetic to you. Why would a grown man need to be taken care of? But I do. I've always had a hard time being practical and organized. Your gran used to tear her hair out about me."

I laughed. That was a funny idea. Dad laughed, too.

Then he said something that really surprised me. "Your mother and I are too much alike."

"*Alike?*" I couldn't help blurting out. "I thought you were too *different*. The kind of music you like and all that."

"We're both dreamers," he said. "I want to play music, and she wants to write. One of us needs to be down to earth. Can you understand that, Lydia?"

Ugh ugh ugh was all I could think. I hereby swear to myself that I will never *never* marry because it is all too stupid for words.

He said, "Your mother didn't want to spend the rest of her life taking care of me, and I guess I can't blame her."

I let this sink in for a minute. The inside of my ears felt hot, and I started to hear a buzzing. "Or me," I squeaked out.

"You?" he asked.

"She didn't want to take care of me. That's why she moved to Minnesota and that's why I'm in boarding school." My throat was achy, and there was a bitter taste in my mouth. The buzzing inside my ears was getting louder. I started to cry. Writing this is making me cry again. I'm using a blood pen to write this, and the writing is getting all blotchy.

Sunday, February 21

It is Sunday morning. I decided to get up this morning and write about the rest of yesterday. I don't feel like crying so much anymore. Yesterday was good, not bad. It was just a relief to cry because I've tried so hard for so long not to.

I am sitting at the desk and trying to write this before April tells me to do homework. Even though I don't have to go back to school until Monday, she wants me to get it out of the way. Collie called and asked if I could do something with her this afternoon. And last night Lacey called. Just to talk. She said she missed me!

This house smells of furniture polish.

Anyhow, to get back to yesterday, I was crying, and Dad pulled the car over to the side of the road. He kept patting my shoulder and saying, "Lyddie, Lyddie." For some reason that made me laugh, so I was laughing *and* crying.

"It wasn't your mother's idea to send you to boarding school," he said. "She didn't want you to go."

I opened the glove compartment and snapped it shut and opened it again and snapped it shut. "Then it was yours and April's. You didn't want to take care of me either."

"Lydia, it was *Gran's* idea." I stopped crying and stared at him. "Before Gran died, she said she would provide money for your schooling at Pocket. She often said she didn't think our idea of splitting the year with you was a good one. She didn't think you were happy in either place, and she was sure you'd be happy at Pocket."

"Well, she was—" I didn't finish the sentence. The word *wrong* caught in my throat. I thought about Gran being Bunny. I could be mad at Gran, but I couldn't be mad at Bunny. I started snapping the glove compartment open and shut again. Dad put a hand out to stop me.

"If you are really miserable, I'm sure we can work something out."

"You mean I don't *have* to go?"

"At the end of this year, we'll take a look at it and decide. How about that?"

I breathed out a big breath. It felt as if a giant snowplow had come and plowed a mountain of bad stuff away. But there was still one bad patch. Well, it was now or never.

I said, "I don't want to take piano lessons."

But I said it too softly, and Dad asked, "What did you say?"

"I don't want to take piano lessons." Each word was this weight that I had to spit out of my mouth. I could see Dad's face out of the corner of my eyes, and he looked as if he still did not understand.

"Are you saying you don't *want* to take piano lessons?"

"I'm not good at the piano." My voice slid up in a wail. I hated the way I sounded, but I couldn't stop. "I like music and everything, but I'm not good at the piano."

"You don't just get good overnight," he said.

"I've been taking piano for six years." I started snapping the glove compartment again.

"Lydia, please don't do that." I dug my nails into my hand. I didn't care what he said or how mad he was at me. I wasn't going to take piano lessons ever again. "Well," he said finally with a big sigh. "What would you like to learn? Or maybe you'd like to take up ballet again?"

"I can't do ballet," I said. "I'm the wrong body type." I couldn't help smiling. I tried to think of what kind of lessons I would like to have. Drawing. It would be neat to learn how to draw better, but Howie could show me how to draw. He was so good at it himself. I could learn how to make water clocks. Who gave lessons in that? Well, Howie. And I was already doing that.

I said to Dad, "I guess I'm not really a lesson kind of person."

"Hmm," he said. "I'm just afraid someday you may wish you'd stuck with it."

"Then I can take lessons again," I said.

"It'll be too late," he said.

I sighed. I knew he was disappointed, but all I could think of was that I, Lydia Rice, will never take another piano lesson in my life. I, Lydia Rice, do not have to go to boarding school if I do not want to.

Dad gave me a little punch and started the car. "Well, we'd better get going if we're going," he said. He turned on the radio. It was a rock-and-roll station. He started singing along with it. I stared at him, and he said, "I don't just like Mozart, you know."

"I didn't know," I said.

He said, "Ha," punched me again, and started singing again.

"Don't do that," I said.

"Why? Am I embarrassing you?" he asked.

"It doesn't seem like you," I said. "You're acting like a kid."

"Aren't I allowed to act like a kid sometimes?" he asked.

"No," I said.

I knew right away when we crossed into New Hampshire because there were more pine trees. There was more snow and not as many cars on the road. It felt quieter. When you cross into New Hampshire, everything bad is left behind. The radio started to come in blurry. Dad turned it off, and I was glad because I like the quiet. Dad was quiet, too, which is more the way he usually is; but now it didn't feel as if there was such a big empty space between us.

Soon we were going down the long dirt road to Gran's house. "Lucky thing for us Mr. Turkell lives on the same road and keeps it plowed," Dad said.

I hadn't been to Gran's house since the Thanksgiving before she died. Two years ago. All these memories came rushing back as I got out of the car and my feet crunched in the snow. Dad opened the front door, and I breathed in all the Hidden Lake house smells. It smelled fresh and musty at the same time, of mothballs and the woodstove, of old books and dried flowers. It was very cold inside, so cold it almost felt as if we were inside an invisible blanket of cold; but it was also very sunny. I had forgotten how the sun comes into Gran's kitchen and how much I like her yellow curtains. She has such a nice view, too. There is a meadow, and your eyes keep moving back until you see the lake, and way back are the mountains.

Right away I wanted to look at Gran's paintings. Now

it is funny to think that Gran probably started to learn how to paint at Pocket. The first one I saw was the one of the view down to the lake and the one of Dad when he was little. He is playing with a toy sailboat at the edge of the lake. With excitement buzzing in my toes and fingers, I headed for the cozy place under the stairs where I knew my favorite painting was.

Dad was saying, "Mice have been having a good time here. But it's amazing to come back! Nothing has changed since I was a boy: the woodstove, the books, the paintings! What a wonderful place this is!"

He was talking on and on. Meanwhile there I was in the cozy place under the stairs where on rainy days, Jip and I would curl up with a blanket and read—at least, I would read, and Jip would sleep. I purposely closed my eyes and didn't look for a moment, and then slowly I opened my eyes and looked at the painting of a girl with blonde hair and rosy cheeks. The girl is a little plump, and she is sitting on a couch. The sun is coming in the window, and she has a white kitten in her lap.

It is Abby Webb with Biscuit.

I looked at the little rabbit in the right-hand corner of the painting. There is a little rabbit with a circle around it. I had looked at that rabbit a thousand times, but I'd never known what it meant before. I had never realized it was the way Gran signed her paintings.

I yelled, "Bunny!" at the top of my lungs.

Dad came running. "What is it?" he asked.

"Bunny," I said. "Gran's nickname."

"Good grief," he said. "Yes, Bunny was Gran's nickname when she was young. I thought you had found a dead animal under the stairs."

"I know who that girl in the painting is," I said. "Her name is Abby Webb, and she was one of Gran's friends. Now she is Mrs. Walker, and I have been over to her house. She lives near Pocket, and she has all these animals."

Dad was nodding. "I think I may have met her a long time ago. I seem to remember she had a lot of dogs."

I laughed. "She still does. What was Gran's name before she got married?"

"Hamilton," said Dad. "You know that—Hamilton is my middle name."

He said he was going across the road to see Mr. Turkell. While he was gone, I looked around the house to see if there were any more things from when Gran was at Pocket. Well, bingo, I found an old photo album crammed in with a lot of old books on one of the bookshelves. A lot of the pictures are brownish-yellow and faded, but there are some pretty good ones of Gran. She has short curly hair, and I do look like her!

In one of the pictures, she is standing next to a girl with long braids. That must be Lizzy. The two girls are wearing sailor-suit tops and bloomers. There is also a picture of Abby Webb, and she is holding Biscuit. In another picture they are standing with a tall man who has a lot of thick black hair. He has a dazzling smile. He looks very handsome. He reminds me of someone, maybe Lacey's father; but I just realized he might be Mr. Pendragon because there is another photo of him standing next to Miss Pocket. At least I'm pretty sure the woman in the long skirt is Miss Pocket. The two of them look so nice, and interesting. I think I would have liked Pocket when they were there.

When Dad came back, I asked him if I could take the album with me. He said yes. I can't wait to show it to Howie and Mrs. Walker. Dad told me Mr. Turkell is going to check on the woodstove and the chimney to make sure they're safe for when Dad comes up for his two weeks. I think it is great Dad is going to do that. He seems much less foggy now.

All in all, it hasn't been bad being with Dad-and-April. But guess what is strange. I can't wait to get back to school!

Tuesday, February 23

Blistering bleeding crustaceans! Everything is wrong! Everything is terrible!

Collie and I got back a few hours ago. As soon as we

stepped through the door, a bomb hit us. Mr. O'Hare, Miss Sparring, Mrs. Fisk, Mr. Wing were waiting for us when we walked in. We are in *so* much trouble.

Now we have to have a big meeting with Mr. Wing. Collie and I are in my room waiting for Lacey to get back. Poor Lacey. It will be the first thing that hits her when she gets back. I don't care for myself, except it's too bad because I was just beginning to like school. The really bad part is about Howie. If they ask me about how we got into the locked buildings, I don't know what I'll say.

I'm probably going to get kicked out. I mean, if Whitney got suspended for smoking a few cigarettes, what are they going to do to someone for stealing the school keys, going into a teacher's closet, and breaking his stuff? Good-bye, Pocket. Good-bye, Lacey, Fish, and Collie. Good-bye, science class. Good-bye, Mrs. Walker. Good-bye, mural. Good-bye, Howie.

I am so stupid and dumb. How could I go and do something like that after everything Howie ever did for me? Even though it makes me feet squirmy to write this, I have to admit I wanted the others to like me. I thought if we didn't go ahead with Operation Pig Heart, they wouldn't.

I just hope Lacey, Collie, and Fish don't get kicked out. I can tell Mr. Wing it was all my idea. That I'm the one who took the keys.

Lacey is here with her father. I have to go.

Later . . .

I'm sitting on my bed waiting for the verdict.

That meeting was the scariest thing I have ever lived through. We all sat in Mr. Wing's office—Mr. Wing; Miss Sparring; Mr. O'Hare; Mrs. Fisk; and Lacey's father, Mr. Sullivan. And then there were Fish, Lacey, Collie, and last but not least, me.

Mr. Wing asked Fish to tell us what happened. Poor Fish. He said, "We got up in the middle of the night and went into Duckworth and went into Mr. O'Hare's closet and accidentally broke his skull. We didn't mean to. We were looking for—we were looking for something else."

Mr. Wing asked, "What was it you were looking for?"

All this electricity zigzagged around the room. My skin felt tight, and I swear my hair was standing straight up on my head. No one said a word.

"Anybody?" said Mr. Wing.

Well, I was lead dog, I had to do the talking.

"A pig heart," I said weakly. "We thought he—Mr. O'Hare—had a pig heart in his closet."

All the grown-ups shifted in their chairs and uncrossed their legs and looked at each other and looked at me. I could feel my face burning. "A pig heart?" asked Mr. Wing.

"The heart of a pig," I said. "Everyone in the school thinks he has—had—one in his closet. We just wanted to find out for sure."

Mr. Sullivan began to laugh. He laughed a jolly-giant laugh. He laughed the electricity right out of the air.

He said in his thick southern accent, "I don't know what y'all want to do about this, but I'm going to tell y'all what I think. I think this was a harmless and innocent kid's prank, and I'll tell y'all something else. [Well, maybe he didn't say y'all so many times.] My daughter, Lacey, here is the happiest I've seen her since her mama passed away. Why, this child opens her mouth and *talks* now. She's making herself some friendships here, and if she's into a little mischief, I take that to be a good sign. Course y'all don't want these girls to be up at all hours of the night, I can see that; and of course I'll respect anything you decide to do about this. I'll just leave it up to you folks." He stood up, this big giant, and walked out of the room.

Miss Sparring said, "There is just one thing, hem-

hem. I would like to know more about how they got into the building."

Here we go, I thought. It's all over. Fish looked at the floor. Collie and Lacey looked at each other. I could tell they were trying not to look at me. Okay, I thought. What am I going to say? How do I tell this but not mention Howie?

"Oh yes, well," Mr. Wing said before I could even open my mouth. "I did go down and speak to our night watchman and tell him students had gotten into Duckworth. He said he had left a set in the door by mistake, didn't know how long he had left them there, and he was sorry about it."

Howie covered up for us!

"Hem-hem, I think the students had better go while we discuss this," Miss Sparring said.

We got out of there as fast as we could.

Lacey ran sobbing into her father's arms. "There, there, honey," he said.

"You're really not mad?" she asked.

"You better believe it, honey," said Mr. Sullivan. "I couldn't be happier."

Fish said, "I'm sorry for telling. Mr. O'Hare forced it out of me." He told us how, over the long weekend while we were gone, Mr. O'Hare had found the broken skull in his closet. He went straight to Fish and accused him. Mr. O'Hare said he figured it was the kind of thing Fish would do. Fish got scared and ended up telling him that he broke it. Mr. O'Hare wanted to know the details, so Fish told him he snuck into Duckworth in the middle of the night.

Mr. O'Hare said, "How? It's locked." Fish didn't know what to say so he said the basement door wasn't locked. Mr. O'Hare said, "But my closet is always locked."

Fish said, "Well, it wasn't."

Mr. O'Hare said, "Yes it was; it always is; you must be lying."

So Fish said, "I found a key."

Mr. O'Hare asked, "Where did you find the key?"

Fish said, "I don't know; I just found it."

"What do you mean, you just found it?" demanded Mr. O'Hare.

Fish said, "We just found it."

"Aha!" cried Mr. O'Hare, "Now it's *we*, is it? Who do you mean by *we*?" Fish didn't say anything, so Mr. O'Hare said, "By *we* do you mean our friend Lydia Rice?" Fish still didn't say anything, and Mr. O'Hare said, "You'd better tell or you will get into worse trouble." Fish ended up telling him it was me, and then he also told about Lacey and Collie. Mr. O'Hare said we (Fish and I) were a bad influence on Lacey and Collie.

Fish was almost crying while he was telling us all this because he felt so bad.

"It's okay," I said. "I don't blame you. I would have

told, too." I feel sorry for him and for Mrs. Fisk. Mr. O'Hare has been so mean to both of them, saying things like Fish has been raised without any discipline.

Fish asked, "How did you get those keys, anyhow?"

My heart began to hammer. I was saved from answering as Mrs. Fisk and Mr. O'Hare came out of Mr. Wing's office. Mr. O'Hare took one look at us and said, "You should not be standing here in the hallway having a party. Alexander, you can wait with your mother in her office. You girls go upstairs, to your own rooms. Mr. Wing will be calling you back down shortly."

On the way up, Mr. Sullivan took Collie's arm and said, "You're coming with us, young lady."

Collie said, "But Mr. O'Hare said I should go to my own room."

"Mr. O'Hare is a fine and worthy gentleman," said Mr. Sullivan. "But this is no time to be isolated as if you were a common criminal." Mr. Sullivan looks and talks like a movie star. It is almost worth being in trouble just to be around him.

When we got back to the room, he spotted Gran's old photo album and asked to see it. Everyone sat on my bed and looked through it. Mr. Sullivan had lots of questions and acted so interested in everything that I almost forgot I was in trouble. When we were looking at the picture of Miss Pocket, I told them how she had started the school for girls so they could learn to draw and paint.

Just then Miss Sparring came into our room and asked Mr. Sullivan to come down to Mr. Wing's office. So he has gone.

I am sitting on my bed writing. It is helping me feel less nervous.

Lacey and Collie both just said the best things. Lacey said, "If we hadn't been so mean, you never would have decided to go through with Operation Pig Heart, and we wouldn't have been in all this trouble. I'm so sorry."

Collie said, "Me, too. We were really being jerky. We thought you were just showing off. We thought you were only pretending you could get the key."

I said, "I do show off a lot. I don't blame you."

No one said anything for a minute, and then Collie said, "Maybe we'll get kicked out like Whitney."

"What happened to Whitney, anyway?" I asked.

"Her parents are sending her to a different boarding school, a much stricter one."

We all looked at each other. I felt a pain in my stomach.

I wonder what Mom is going to say about all of this. I know Dad will be mad, but Mom? Mom might laugh and think it's funny. I wish Mom weren't so far away.

Lacey said, "You're not really a show-off, Lydia. My father says you have a lot of spirit. And you know what? It's kind of good what happened because I found out I could be mean."

I said, "I like knowing you can be mean because I used to think you were so good you made me feel bad."

Lacey grinned, and I felt as if I had said the right thing. Then she started to giggle that wicked giggle of hers and said, "I just keep remembering Fish in that hat and that dress."

"You looked pretty funny in that leopard outfit," I said. We all started to laugh. Even though I'm in trouble, I'm happy because I feel as if Lacey and Collie are really my friends now.

The only thing is this bad pricking I feel whenever I think about Howie. He must know I took the keys.

Oh boy, Mr. Sullivan just came in and told us to go down to the lion's den. He said, "Thumbs up, girls," and winked a big movie-star wink. I guess that means good news. Maybe we're not going to be expelled? Just suspended?

Later . . .

We sat down in Mr. Wing's office. Everyone was in there again. It was hard to breathe.

Mr. Wing said, "Well, we have discussed this and are in agreement with Mr. Sullivan that there was no malicious intent. On the whole we are not inclined to take this too seriously. It all could be an incident from *Tom Sawyer*, ha-ha-ha-ha, but . . . "

Then he frowned and looked straight at me. I thought he was going to say, "Except in Lydia's case."

"But," he went on, "being up after hours is against the rules, going out of the dormitory after hours is against the rules, rummaging through a teacher's closet is an invasion of property, and not reporting the damage is dishonest, and perhaps, cowardly."

He took a deep breath. "So we have misdemeanors on a number of levels. Therefore, you are all grounded until the end of the winter term. You are not to leave campus except for church and school outings. You will make reparations to Mr. O'Hare in the form of physical labor. You will shovel snow, chop ice, sweep the dining rooms, and wash the blackboards. You will write a letter of apology to Mr. O'Hare. And, if you are ever caught out of your rooms after hours again, there will be severe consequences."

Everyone was quiet.

Mr. Wing said, "You may go now."

Fish, Lacey, Collie, and I burst out of there. We ran as fast as we could down the stairs, just to be as far away from Mr. Wing's office as we could get. We ended up near the mural. I touched Gran, just to be near her.

"They let us off!" Fish said.

"All because of your dad, Lacey," I said.

"You won't be able to go to Mrs. Walker's anymore," Lacey said to me.

"That's nothing," I said. "Poor Collie won't be able to go to any more dances this term."

"I hate them anyway," she said.

"You *do?*" we all shouted, and then we laughed and hugged each other. We even hugged Fish.

Collie asked, "What was that skull, anyway? Was it a human skull?"

Fish said, "No, it was his horse when he was a kid."

We all stood there in stunned silence.

"It was his favorite horse," said Fish. "That's why he was so upset."

We stood there and shuddered.

But anyway, it's over. Well, no it's not. It's not over until I can talk to Howie.

Later . . .

Mom actually called! It was so good to hear her voice. It made me cry. She has heard about everything. She laughed about the pig heart and the skull. She said I should write it all down, that it all would make a great story. I told her I did write it down. She said good, send it to her. Hearing her voice makes everything seem better, that she does love me. She says she can't wait for me to come out for spring vacation.

Right after I got off the phone with Mom, Dad called. He said he hoped I understood I had no business prowling around the school in teachers' closets. I said yes. It wasn't that great a conversation. I think Dad was madder about it than Mr. Wing.

After that I called Mrs. Walker. I told her about getting into trouble. She thought the pig heart thing was really funny. I told her I was grounded for the rest of the winter term. She said she would come by soon and visit. I wanted to tell her about Howie and the keys, but I couldn't get the words out. Not on the phone, anyway.

I want to go down after lights-out, but I'm too scared. I'll get into wicked trouble if I get caught.

I want to tell Howie that it wasn't so bad being with Dad-and-April. I want to tell him that Dad is happy because he's going to play in the symphony. I want to tell him I'm doing better in school. I want to tell him how I'm really getting along with Lacey, Collie, and Fish.

And, I want to tell him about Operation Pig Heart so he understands why I took the keys.

Later . . .

I am so worried.

I decided that I had to break the rules and go find Howie. I waited until so, so late because I knew Miss Hammer would be lying in wait for me. I made it down the stairs. The Silly Wizard sign is gone. I was just going to knock on Howie's door when a strange man came out and asked, "What are you doing?"

I couldn't say anything. I was completely frozen. The man said, "You're not supposed to be up, are you?" He was carrying a flashlight and a bunch of keys, just like Howie always did, but he was not Howie. "Do you have some sort of problem?" he asked.

I said no, it was nothing, and ran back upstairs to my room as fast as I could.

Wednesday, February 24

I spent the whole day looking for Howie. I couldn't find him anywhere. I went by his room a million times. I walked all over the school, looking for him. I asked everyone if they had seen him, even Nellie in the kitchen. No one knew where he was. Nellie said she hadn't seen him for a few days, but she also said, "Sometimes he's like that. He has his good days and his bad days."

I went to see Mr. Wing. I figured the headmaster of the school would know about the maintenance man and the night watchman.

Miss Farrow, his secretary, said I could go in.

"Ah, hello, Lydia," he said when he saw me. "Would you like to look in my closet? Got a few skeletons in there, ha-ha! But no hearts, ha-ha! Now what can I do for you?"

I took a deep breath and said, "I was wondering about Howie, the maintenance man. Is he okay? I mean, I haven't seen him around. I was wondering if what we did made him not want to work here anymore."

Mr. Wing nodded and said, "Well, Lydia, Howie, as you might have noticed, is an elderly man, and not always in the best of health. When Howie realized he had misplaced the keys, he was very upset. He came straight to me and said he had never done anything like that before. He said it was a sure sign he wasn't up to the job anymore. He requested immediate leave."

There was this awful churning in my stomach. I sat and dug my nails into my legs. Mr. Wing kept talking and talking, oh so cheerfully, as if he were telling me about his vacation in Florida or something.

"I urged him to stay on. He is such a nice old fellow, very loyal to the school, knows everything about it, and he is so handy—able to fix anything, you know. I was a bit concerned when some years back he asked, in addition to his maintenance duties, to take on being the night watchman. I thought it might be a bit much for him. I wondered when was he going to sleep, but he said he didn't need much sleep. He'd catch a wink between shifts, which would be plenty enough for him. To tell the truth, Lydia, I didn't press him. He is a private man. After all, Pocket has been his home. I mean, not many of us can say we have actually taught with Miss Pocket."

I felt the room sort of lurch.

"He *taught* with Miss Pocket?" I asked.

Mr. Wing nodded. "Yes, indeed. There he is." He pointed to a framed photograph on his wall. It was a lot like the one Gran had in her album, of the tall, handsome art teacher with the thick black hair standing next to Miss Pocket. "He is a veritable walking encyclopedia of Pocket history. Of course I allowed him to stay on."

I stood up and went over and stared and stared at the photograph. Okay, I could see it now. Those were Howie's eyes, his nose. My legs were shaking so badly I thought I was going to fall over. My throat was closed up, and my mouth was dry. A hundred thoughts were clattering around inside my skull.

Howie was Mr. Pendragon. Why hadn't I guessed that?

I knew he had known the Pocket girls—Lizzy and Abby, Dottie and Connie—and Bunny. He had known my grandmother. But I hadn't ever thought much about *how* he had known them. I had always thought of him as Howie, the way he is now. I never imagined him being young, romantic, and handsome.

The old days at Pocket and Mr. Pendragon were all part of a fairy tale, a story—not *real*.

"Do you know where he is?" I asked weakly.

Mr. Wing shook his head. "That I don't," he said. "It's nice of you to show such an interest, Lydia. You must have struck up a friendship with him. He could be very nice with you girls."

"I don't want—I don't want what I did to be the reason for him leaving."

Now, you dummy, tell him. Tell him you took the keys from Howie.

Oh, why why why, blistering, bleeding crustaceans, why couldn't I tell him? *I kept wanting to, so why couldn't I?*

Mr. Wing was saying, "Most probably he was ready to go. It was really too much of a job for one old man. Every time I saw him out there shoveling, my conscience plagued me. Yes, it's going to require *two* men to fill his shoes—a maintenance man *and* a night watchman."

"I *have* to find him," I said.

"Oh dear, Lydia, you certainly do seem upset. Well, why don't you speak to Mr. Hunter, the business manager. He is sure to have Howie's address and so on." Since I didn't move, Mr. Wing cleared his throat and asked, "Is there anything else, Lydia?"

I shook my head. How could I tell him that inside my head I was picturing a pretty woman with long, dark hair. She was Dorothea Ehrenhaft—Dottie—and Howie had been married to her.

"And now, Miss Rice," said Mr. Wing, sounding like a headmaster, "you should get back to business. I understand you are doing very much better in your studies."

Staggering out of his office, I looked around. The halls were empty. Everyone was in classes, but I wasn't ready to get back to business. I drifted into the sitting room, sank onto the couch, and tried to breathe. Miss Pocket looked down at me. For the first time I noticed the small rabbit in the lower right-hand corner of the portrait.

"Oh, Gran," I thought, my eyes pricking. "I should have known." It was the portrait I liked. And then I thought, Howie was the person who taught Gran how to paint.

I looked at the clock on the wall. History class was going on. I didn't care. Right then and there I had to go find Mr. Hunter, the business manager, and get Howie's address. I went back to Miss Farrow's desk and asked her if I could see Mr. Hunter.

Mr. Hunter's door was open, and he was sitting at his desk. I'd seen him around but had never known before what he did. For one thing, he looks like a gangster. He wears a gray three-piece suit, a big ring with a stone in it on his little finger, and his hair is all slicked back.

He looked up as I just sort of stood in his doorway. "Hello there, little lassie," he said in a big, booming voice. "How can I help you? Come in, come in; it's all right. I don't bite."

I went a little way in. I could barely breathe because of the cologne he was wearing.

"Mr. Wing said you would have Howie's address," I said. "Howie, the maintenance man."

"Well, little lassie, he virtually lived here, you know. I don't recall that he had another address."

"But where is he *now*?" I asked.

"Well, sorry to say, I don't know," said Mr. Hunter. "He just up and left."

"You mean, you don't have any idea where he might be?"

Mr. Hunter got up from his desk and rummaged through a file cabinet. He finally turned to me and said, "Well, little lassie, I don't seem to be having much luck. I expect he'll turn up. He wouldn't just never come back here again."

I left his office and didn't know what to do because I sure didn't want to go to history class. But I did go, and when I got there Mr. O'Hare made me go back to Miss Farrow. I had to ask her to write a note saying I was with Mr. Wing and Mr. Hunter. It was dumb because it just meant I missed even more of his class.

I feel as if I am in a dark hole, and I will never come out of it.

Thursday, February 25

During recess today I stopped by my cubbie, and there was a letter.

It was from Howie. I recognized his handwriting on the envelope. It is very fancy with lots of curls. I started reading it right there in front of the cubbies, and that was a mistake. I didn't want to cry in front of everyone. I went up to my room, but Mrs. Prokopovich saw me and said, "Sorry, duck, you're not supposed to be in here during the day." I grabbed my diary because I have to talk about this with someone, and now I am sitting under the stairs, next to my water clock.

Howie said he is sorry he left so suddenly without telling me.

He said when Mr. Wing came to him about some kids going into Duckworth and getting into Mr. O'Hare's closet, he knew of course that it was me; and he realized I must have taken his keys without asking.

He said he should never have—*O bleeding blast*. I can't write this!! Basically Howie thought making friends with me was a mistake, but he couldn't help being drawn to Bunny's granddaughter.

Then he said, "Lydia, continue your Silly Wizard task. I set this particular challenge for you for a reason, and you should finish what you've begun. When you have finished, go out under the moon and become transformed, not into a penguin, but into yourself. My wish for you is that you become your true self, a self your gran would have been proud of. You have given this Silly Wizard some fine moments. The water clock is underneath the stairs, by the way, across from the mural. *Rach manji*, Lydia."

And inside the envelope was another Silly Wizard story.

Laura, Once a Girl

Miss Howl had no patience with the boy Martin. Perhaps it was because Martin had once been a mouse, and the owl in Miss Howl had sniffed him out. One day she sent him home for not raising his hand.

"She can't send him home for not raising his hand," a flustered Mrs. Morning said to Mr. Old. "She can't send him home *at all*. Only I can do that."

Mr. Old pulled on his beard. She was a worrisome creature, this Miss Howl, and it was his fault she was there. His only hope was that the daffodils were up and the trees were leafing out. It was the time of year when teachers were rehired. Mr. Old was hoping Mrs. Morning would not rehire Miss Howl, but of course, it was not his place to say.

But Mrs. Morning *did* rehire Miss Howl. She was afraid not to.

With the coming of spring, the days grew warm. And on the surface of Michael's scalp, little shoots of green hair began to appear.

At first the hair was the tender green of spring's early leaves. Then as it began to fill out and lengthen, Michael developed a head of thick, dark green hair. As a matter of fact, it was the same color as Laura's sweater.

"Hey, that's neat-o," said all the seventh graders. The next day all the seventh graders came to school with their hair dyed green, every one that is except for Laura.

Mrs. Morning sat down with Michael. "Michael," she said, "you are a natural leader, and the other students look up to you. Look at what you have done!"

"It just started to grow," said Michael. "It just started to grow; and when it did, it was green. It is spring, after all. In the fall I suppose it will turn red." He smiled, and little smile lines appeared around his eyes.

"Spring," Mrs. Morning echoed softly. "Of course, it is spring. Why shouldn't your hair be green." She smiled back at him and found herself not caring at all that his hair was green. For that matter she liked the way some of the others looked with green hair, Martin, in particular. For some reason he looked less mousy.

Laura came to Michael a few days later. "I would like to become a tree," she said. "What do I have to do?"

"You have to go outside on a moonlit night and find a Silly Wizard," said Michael. "But why would you want to do that?"

"Trees aren't stuck up. They don't care if you are different," said Laura. "Now the kids are all giving me a hard time because I won't dye my hair green. I am going to find a Silly Wizard tonight."

"I'll miss you," said Michael.

"Well, I won't go very far. I can be a maple in the

middle of the courtyard. We need a tree there, anyway. Do you think I can find a Silly Wizard?"

Michael assured her that she could if she just went outside and waited for a while. So that night, Laura stood nervously beneath the moon. Mr. Old came by and saw her there.

"What are you doing outside, Laura?" he asked.

Laura instantly recognized the Silly Wizard in Mr. Old. "I'd like to be a maple tree," she said.

"Well," he said. "Are you sure? You seem like a nice girl to me."

"Yes, I'm sure. I've actually been thinking about this for a long time."

"My spells have come out a bit sillier than usual lately," said Mr. Old. "But I'll see what I can do."

Mr. Old paced back and forth, back and forth, and finally he began to mutter under his breath. Laura heard him say, "Sap from the South, new leaves from the North." But then she thought she heard him say, "Elegant pattern from the East." *What?* What was he talking about? And then last of all, she heard, "Wings from the West."

Laura wanted to cry out, "Trees don't have wings," but Mr. Old was already commanding her to shut her eyes, hold up her arms, and stretch.

Trembling with uncertainty, Laura held up her arms and stretched. She felt herself shrinking. "But I should be growing," she thought. And then her arms seemed to be waving threadlike in the air. She opened her eyes. She was very close to the ground. "This is not right," she thought. "What am I?"

"A beetle!" she heard Michael exclaim. He happened to have been waiting in the shadows, watching everything. He stepped out now. "O Silly Wizard!" he cried. "What have you done?"

"I couldn't quite remember the charm," said Mr. Old meekly. "I'm so sorry. The best I could manage was a beetle that lives in maple trees. Won't that do?"

"No!" Michael shouted.

"I beg your pardon," said Mr. Old, suddenly feeling very old. He pressed a hand against his heart.

"Oh, please, it's really all right," said Michael, who had a soft heart and didn't like to see the Silly Wizard upset. He hurriedly scooped Laura the beetle into his hand. "I'm sure she'll be just as happy as a beetle."

Michael put the beetle into a glass jar with some new young maple leaves and twigs taken from a tree in front of the school. He kept the jar on his desk.

During recess the two most popular girls in the seventh grade came into the classroom. Jessica picked up the jar and peered into it. "Look at this bug of Michael's," she said. "It's got this pretty design on its back."

"Michael seems kind of quiet, though, don't you think?" Marie asked, also peering into the jar.

"He probably misses Laura," said Jessica jealously. "I don't see what he sees in her. Where is she, anyway?"

"I don't know," said Marie, "but I think she's brave."

There was silence in the room before Jessica asked, "You do?"

"I kind of look up to her. She does what she wants. Like wearing that green sweater and not dyeing her hair when everyone else did. I'm always trying to please people so they'll like me."

"Yeah, I guess I'm like that, too," said Jessica.

They were both quiet, staring at the bug. The bug, for her part, had overheard everything. She was so happy she wanted to crawl right out of the jar. The lid, however, was screwed on tightly.

Laura thought about what she should do. When Michael came back to his desk, she tried tapping her antennae against the glass, but he didn't hear her. She tried flying up and thwumping her little body against the lid, but he wasn't paying attention. In desperation she set about chewing tiny little letters into the maple leaves: I WANT TO BE A GIRL AGAIN.

It took Michael until afternoon study hall to notice. He happened to rest his head on the desk. His nose was next to the jar, and the curve of the glass happened to magnify the leaf letters. He sat straight up and shouted, and naturally got into trouble with Miss Howl. But he didn't care. His best friend, Laura, wanted to be a girl again.

The night finally came. Michael released Laura the beetle just as Mr. Old stepped out into the courtyard to begin his rounds.

"Come here, Silly Wizard," commanded Michael. "You have a job to do."

"Another one?" Mr. Old asked doubtfully. He was beginning to wonder if he was losing his touch.

"Bend down to the ground and listen to that beetle," said Michael.

"Silly Wizard," the beetle called in a small, crackly voice. "Please make me a girl again."

Mr. Old heaved a sigh of relief. This he could do.

"Beetle wings now quickly unfurl
So that you can now be a girl."

He nearly shouted the charm, so happy was he that Laura wanted to come back. Laura found herself growing rapidly, all her human sensations returning. She stood in the courtyard, a girl again, albeit a bit dizzy.

"Phew," said both Michael and Mr. Old.

Michael put out a hand to hold her steady. "Am I glad to see you," he said. He looked at her anxiously. "Are you glad to be a girl again?"

"Yes," said Laura. She breathed in the spring air and smiled at Michael, his green hair glowing as if he were some kind of firefly. "I'm glad to be *Laura*," she emphasized.

I guess I know why he wrote that story.

Recess is over. No more feet tramping over my head.

I am looking at the mural that Howie painted. I made him quit! I don't think he has money to live on. I don't know if he has a house to live in, or anything.

Mr. O'Hare must be wondering where I am. What am I going to do? I don't want to go to class.

I am looking at Bunny—at Gran. What should I *do*, Gran? I wish she were still alive and I could be in that tree with her.

What am I going to do?

You know what? I have a brilliant idea.

Later . . .

I am in the maple tree in the courtyard now. I went up to my room and put on two sweaters and my winter jacket, pajama bottoms, ski pants, hat, scarf, and mittens—and I am still cold. This time I remembered a flashlight. I brought *Jane Eyre* and this diary. I am so glad Gran gave it to me. I am writing in it with a blood pen.

Later . . .

Classes just changed. All these girls came by. At first no one noticed me. That was a strange feeling. It made me feel invisible. Then Bix Potter stopped and looked up. She asked, "What are you doing up there?"

I said, "I'm staying up here until Howie comes back."

"Who is Howie?" she asked.

"*Who is Howie?*" I shouted. I was furious. "He only does everything around here. Howie, the maintenance man."

"Oh yeah, *Howie*. That nice old guy. He got my locker open for me once when it was jammed. Where'd he go, anyway?"

"He quit!" I shouted, furious.

Mr. O'Hare came across the courtyard. He stood looking up at me for a minute and then said, "What sort of nonsense is this? Come down from there immediately."

I said, "I'm not coming down until Howie comes back and works for Pocket again."

A pretty big crowd was gathering at the bottom of the tree.

"The rest of you get to your classes," Mr. O'Hare snapped. He went away, and it was quiet in the courtyard until he came back with Mr. Wing and Miss Sparring.

Miss Sparring said, "Haven't we, hem-hem, caused enough trouble for one week?"

Mr. Wing said, "What is all this about Howie coming back?"

I said, "I am not coming down until Howie comes back to work for Pocket."

"Come down, Lydia, and we will talk about it," said Mr. Wing.

I said, "When I see Howie working here again, I will come down."

They all stood looking up at me for a minute, and then Mr. O'Hare said, "She'll tire of it."

They went away.

I have been trying to get comfortable in the tree. If I lean back carefully, I can rest and not fall, but I have to be careful not to shift around too much. I'm going to try to read *Jane Eyre*.

Fish just came by. He climbed up into the tree with a thermos. It had hot soup in it. It tasted so good. He also gave me some bread.

"Why are you up here?" he asked.

"I want Howie to come back."

"Howie?"

"You know who Howie is. He did maintenance, and he was the night watchman, too. I can't believe no one has even noticed that he's not here anymore."

"Well, he seemed like a nice guy, but he *was* old. Did he retire or what?"

"He left because of me."

"Because of you?"

"I did something, and I can't tell you yet."

Fish jumped down and said, "Okay, you don't have to tell me. A bunch of us are placing bets, you know. On how long you'll stay. We each put in a dollar and wrote down how long. Whoever gets the closest wins the money."

"Well, I certainly hope *you* win, Fish," I said sarcastically.

"I'll tell you what my bet was," he said hopefully.

"Fish, I don't have any idea how long I'm going to be up here," I said furiously.

Then he had to go, and I was glad because even when he's trying to be nice he really drives me crazy.

Mrs. Prokopovich just came by. She looked up and said, "I simply had to see you with my own two eyes. You'll catch your death up there."

She left, and then Nellie came out. I've never seen Nellie outside of the kitchen. It was strange to see her in boots and a winter coat. She said, "This is a good thing you're doing. Howie needs Pocket. I'll cook you up something hot so you don't freeze to death. It's about time someone cared about that poor old man. You're a good girl."

Thank you, Nellie. Even though I'm not good; and I drove Howie away. Thank you for saying that.

Fish just did a very strange thing. He sort of tiptoed up to the tree, all hunched over like a sneaky spy in a cartoon. He took something out of his pocket and stuffed it into the hollow place in the trunk of the tree. When I was sure no one was around, I climbed down and found a wadded up piece of paper. I opened it up. It was in code.

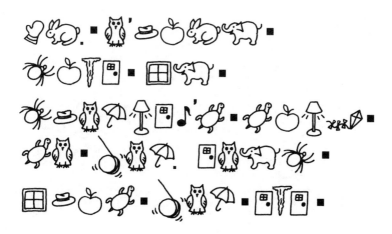

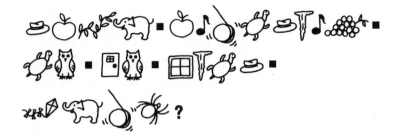

It's getting dark. I'm trying to write before it gets totally dark. I think it's going to be too hard to write and hold a flashlight. A little while ago when no one was around, I climbed down, stretched, and walked around for a bit. I snuck into Pocket Hall and went to the bathroom. Phew. I thought I was going to explode. I hope Howie comes pretty soon. I don't know how long I can keep this up. Anyhow, when I came back, I noticed some white things in the hollow place. My heart leaped. There were two messages.

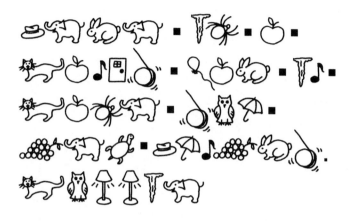

I saw the girls get on the bus for basketball. The bus takes them to a different school because Pocket doesn't have a basketball court. I saw the girls go into our gym for modern dance. I can sort of hear the corny music from here. At least I'm missing that.

Everyone just came out of the gym. Even if they aren't supposed to, they all said, "Hi, Lydia," as if my being up here is the most normal thing in the world. I am holding the flashlight and writing because it keeps me company. La-la-la-la. I am singing to myself. Lights are on in all the windows. I can hear all the radios blaring.

Everything is brick or concrete or glass. I am sitting on the only living thing here. I wish I could turn into a squirrel or something so I could be in this tree and not fall out. If Howie were a real Silly Wizard, I could ask him to turn me into a squirrel. While the girls are having supper, I am going to come down from the tree and go into Pocket Hall and warm up for a minute.

Nellie just brought me a bowl of hot soup and a mug of hot chocolate. I said, "Thank you, Nellie. How long have you been at Pocket?"

"Twenty-two years," she said.

"Gosh," I said. "Did you know Howie all those years?"

"Every one of 'em," she said. "And this year's the happiest I've seen him in a long time. You make him happy, girl, keeping him company."

"Do you think he might come back, Nellie?"

She shook her head. "There's no knowing what he'll do. But you keep up the good work. You're a good girl."

Everyone just went across the courtyard to go to study hall.

Lacey left me a note and her teddy bear.

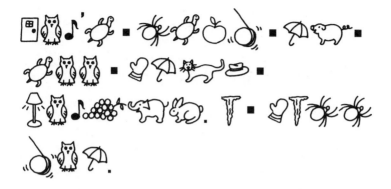

Fish dumped a sleeping bag at the bottom of the tree.
And a note.

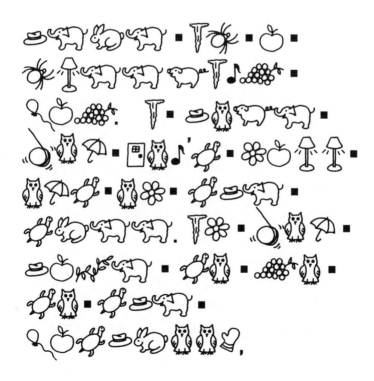

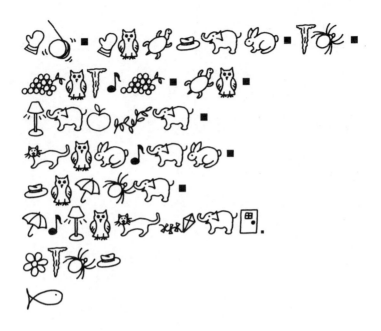

He also left more food from Mrs. Fisk—a peanut-butter-and-jelly sandwich and some cookies, which I ate in about two seconds, and a thermos of hot chocolate. The sandwich made me think of Mom. Before I ate it, I took a bite and pretended Mom had made it. I pretended it was Mom's way of saying everything is going to be okay. Sometimes you have to be your own mom.

I am in the sleeping bag in the tree. I feel like a giant caterpillar in a cocoon. At least the sleeping bag is a little bit soft. I am much warmer now. Mr. Wing came out.

"Lydia," he said, "I'd really like you to come down out of that tree."

"I can't," I said.

"I'm going to have to call your father. Why don't you get out of the tree before he arrives?"

"Have you found Howie?" I asked.

"Can't you tell me why this is so important to you?"

I felt like screaming at him. How could any human being be so dense? "Howie loved Pocket," I said. "He's been here forever." I felt as if I were talking to a little kid who had to have everything spelled out for him. "I don't think he should have left. I'm afraid he'll be really sad if he's not here. And the school needs him, too."

"I'm sure he's fine, Lydia. He wouldn't have left if he didn't want to leave."

"*He's not fine!*" I was shouting now. "*And he didn't want to leave!*"

Mr. Wing shook his head and looked at me for a minute. Then he shook his head again and went back inside.

All the outside flood lights have come on. It's not dark out here at all anymore. I wish Mr. Wing didn't have to call Dad, who is probably at Gran's house trying to play music. He is going to be upset about being interrupted.

The stupid new night watchman just came by. He stopped below the tree and asked, "How ya doin'?"

I said, "Okay."

"Cold enough for ya?" he asked.

"Yup," I said.

"Crazy girl," he said.

Friday, February 26

It is the next day. I actually made it through the night.
I came down from the tree and took the sleeping bag
and blankets into Corner House and curled up in the
bathroom. I kept waking up because I didn't want to be
caught there in the morning, but at least it was warm.
Mrs. Fisk is saving my life. What would Mr. O'Hare say if
he knew what she has been doing for me?

I am back in the tree now. I was hoping Howie would
be here. I'm cold and tired and miserable.

The girls have just come by on their way to morning
assembly. They said, "Hi, Lydia," as if I live here. I am
thinking about all the work I am going to have to make
up. If they let me make it up. Maybe if I come down from
this tree, they will kick me out of school. Maybe I will
have to go live with Mom or Dad. Who will I live with?
Mom? Or Dad? Maybe I'll split the year again. I really
don't want to have to do that.

*   *   *

Guess who came? Dr. and Mrs. Walker. Mrs. Walker brought me a picnic basket full of food. She said Mr. Wing called them because he realized that Mrs. Walker actually knew Howie. Of course! He would have been her teacher years and years ago.

"Poor Mr. Pendragon," she said.

"Did you know he was here as the maintenance man?" I asked.

"Oh yes, I did know, of course. I'd see him every time I came by, you know. We'd chat and gossip about people we used to know, but after a while it grew more and more awkward. I think he was embarrassed to see people who had known him in the old days. He was so talented, you know. He and Dottie were so bright and beautiful, and had so much promise. They created a school together, a small experimental one out in the country, and it was just wonderful. They ran it for years and years, and then poor Dottie got cancer. She was so ill. When she died, poor Mr. Pendragon fell apart. And now he's just disappeared. Well, perhaps he was ready to stop working."

"He wasn't ready," I said. I told them how I had become friends with him, and he had trusted me.

"He must have felt as if he were talking to Bunny sometimes," said Mrs. Walker. "Now that I know who you are, it's hard for me to believe I didn't see the resemblance right away. You *are* so much like her!"

"I did a really bad thing," I said. I sort of gasped, getting the words out, and started to cry, right there up in that tree.

Mrs. Walker looked alarmed. "Oh dear, what on earth could you have done that was so bad?"

So I told them. I told them how I had taken the keys because of Operation Pig Heart. I told them how Howie had lied about leaving the keys in the lock just to cover for me. I told them he probably felt he couldn't work at Pocket anymore. I told them I was pretty sure he needed to have this job, and I wasn't going to come down until he came back.

They didn't say anything at first.

I put my head down so I wouldn't have to look at them. I have never been so ashamed of anything in my life. I felt as if they hated me. If they walked away in total disgust, I wouldn't blame them.

But Dr. Walker asked, "Is anyone actually trying to find him?"

I said, "I don't know."

He left for a minute and came back with a chair. Then he left again, and Mrs. Walker sat down.

"I should have brought my knitting," she said with a laugh.

She sat there and didn't lecture me or tell me what a bad person I was. Instead she told me every story she could remember about the old days. She said Gran had more energy than any person she had ever known. Mr. Pendragon sometimes threatened to tie her to her chair if she didn't sit still. But when she was drawing and painting, she was as still as a mouse. I told her about Gran's house in New Hampshire and about the painting of her that is under the stairs. Mrs. Walker said she had visited that house a number of times and had seen the picture. I asked, "You really have been to Hidden Lake?" She nodded and said she just loved the view from the kitchen.

She stayed for about an hour, and then she had to leave. I love thinking about Mrs. Walker being at Gran's house. I love knowing she has seen things that I have seen. The next time I go and stand in Gran's kitchen, I will think about Mrs. Walker standing in the same place and looking out the window at the view. That is, if I ever get out of this tree.

The best thing is now that I have confessed to the Walkers, I feel lighter, as if maybe there's some hope that Howie might come back.

It was just recess, and Lacey came and sat in the chair. It's nice having visitors, and it's not so cold out today. I'm glad. This is hard. Mr. O'Hare came by, and from the way he was frowning, I thought for a minute he was going to make Lacey leave. But he just frowned some more and went away.

*   *   *

Oh boy, guess what! Dad is here. I actually saw him arrive. I can see the street in front of Pocket House pretty well from up here. I saw his car, and I saw him climb out of it. April is *not* with him. Phew. My heart is just about dropping out of me.

Dad came out to the tree. He climbed right up into it and sat with me! Just as I thought, he said he had been up at Gran's. He asked me if what I was doing was really necessary. I said yes. I thought he was going to be so, so, so mad, but he said, "Well, tell me about it."

I told him everything. About making friends with Howie and his being so nice to me and how I wasn't so homesick after that. I told him about Howie setting the Silly Wizard task. I told him a little about the Silly Wizard stories and also how Howie helped me with my water clock. I explained all about the mural and how I'd figured out who everyone was. It was especially fun telling him about Gran. I told him that in the mural she is in the tree—*this* tree. Dad leaned his head against the trunk, and his eyes got full.

He said, "She sat here in this tree."

Then I told him the bad part.

Talking to Dad took a long time. It passed the time, and I liked having him in the tree with me.

Finally he said, "I'm sorry you took those keys, Lydia, very, very sorry. But now I think you're doing the right

thing. I hope your headmaster can find Howie." Then he
said, "I'm going now, but I'll be back. I'm staying with
the Walkers."

"I hope you like dogs," I said. He smiled.

Fish brought my books and my homework. The
teachers have decided if I'm not going to come down,
then I'd better do my work in the tree! Fish put everything into a basket and tied it to a branch, so all I have to
do to get my history book is reach in. It's kind of funny, if
you ask me.

Later . . .

Gosh, I have a lot to write about.

I don't even know if I can, I am so jumpy. But here
I go.

I was sitting in the tree, and it was getting dark again.
I didn't know if I could keep going. Dad hadn't come
back, or Mrs. Walker, or even Mr. Wing. I thought maybe
this was going to be my punishment—they were just
going to leave me and not talk to me anymore.

And then I heard voices coming from around the corner of Pocket House. First Dad came, and then Dr. Walker
and Mrs. Walker, and then Mr. Wing. They came and stood
beneath the tree.

"Lydia," said Mr. Wing, "you can come down out of the tree now."

"But Howie—" I said.

"Howie is here," said Mr. Wing. "He is waiting for you inside."

"Where was he? How did you find him?"

"He was staying with Nellie's brother."

"Nellie's *brother*?"

"He often went there, I guess. He had a sort of room over the garage. It took a while for the brother to tell Nellie, because Howie didn't want anyone to know where he was. When Nellie told us, it took a while for us to convince Howie to come back. Mrs. Walker did the convincing, actually."

When I climbed down out of the tree, I was all shaky. I started to cry. Mr. Wing kept telling me to go into the day students' lunchroom, that Howie would meet me in there, and that when I was finished I should go and meet them all in Mr. Wing's office.

I made myself put one foot in front of the other. For one thing I was cold and stiff all over. For another, now that Howie was actually here, I was scared to see him. I pulled open the heavy Pocket House door and there he was, sitting on a bench at one of the long tables in the lunchroom, just as if he'd never been gone. He looked thin and kind of worn. I started crying again when I saw him. I couldn't help it.

"I'm sorry," I said. "I'm sorry I took the keys, Mr. Pendragon," I added in a whisper.

"You can call me Howie," he said gruffly.

"No," I said. "You're Mr. Pendragon."

He said, "Sit down, Lydia."

I sat down on the bench opposite him.

"They want me to teach shop. They say girls should learn how to hammer nails and measure and saw. Practical things."

I leaped up off the bench. "They should, Howie, they should! And you'd be the best at teaching it." I was too excited to call him Mr. Pendragon.

"They want me to work in the alumnae office, contacting former students."

I ran around to the other side of the table and shook him by his arm. "That's perfect, Howie."

"They want me to live on the top floor of Corner House. In return for all the years I've worked for Pocket. They want me to keep fiddling around and fixing things, even though they've hired a real maintenance man. Charity for a broken-down old man, I'd say."

I walked back around and sat down on the bench again. I was panicked that he would be too proud to accept their offer. I hardly dared to breathe.

"I said I'd come back on one condition," he said.

"What?" I asked in a small voice.

"That Lydia Rice keeps working on the task I set her."

There was a wicked gleam in his eyes. I breathed more easily now. He was going to take the offer.

"I'm sorry," I said again. "It's the worst thing I've ever done. If you hadn't come back, I'd have hated myself forever."

"I know," he said. He was smiling, his eyes all crinkly. I swear he came back more for me than for himself.

Saturday, February 27

I am at Dad-and-April's now. I have been suspended for a week for stealing the keys.

I am so happy I got a punishment. I couldn't stand the guilt anymore.

I have to work this whole week because Dad-and-April didn't want me to feel as if I'm on vacation. I am working at a place where poor people go and get food and clothing. It makes me think about Howie, how he was sort of a homeless person. Every time I think about how things might have turned out for him, I turn hot and cold. I want to hide under my bed and never come out.

I talked to Mom on the phone for almost two hours. I told her everything. She is the best listener. She kept saying, "Write it down; Lydia, you'll be so glad you did."

I told her I had written it all down in the diary Gran gave me.

Sunday, February 28

Something amazing happened to me.

Dad called me into his study. He said, "Lydia, I have something important to tell you. I have been waiting for the right time to tell you. Well, this past year I think you have grown up considerably, and I believe the time has come. It concerns Gran's will." Dad cleared his throat, and then he told me.

It is almost hard for me to write it down. It is as if something warm and wonderful has been wrapped around me. There is no way I can get that feeling down on paper.

Gran gave me her house.

Hidden Lake belongs to me.

Gran wrote in her will that Lydia Rice, granddaughter of Louise Hamilton Rice, would inherit the Hidden Lake house.

Thinking about going home to Hidden Lake is like thinking about climbing into my own heart.

Thursday, March 4

I have been thinking. Mom wants me to go out to Minnesota for spring vacation. Dad-and-April want me to come here. Lacey wants me to go home with her to Georgia. Mrs. Walker wants me to come and stay for a while.

What if I say I am going home? I mean, to my home? And anyone who wants to come visit me—well, they can.

Friday, March 5

Dad-and-April have been nice to me while I've been here.

They were sitting in the living room when I went in and said, "Dad, I have been thinking."

He said, "Uh-oh, that's dangerous." I told him my idea about Hidden Lake. He looked at me for a solid minute. I know because the grandfather clock was behind him, and I watched the minute hand bounce. Then he said, "April and I would like to visit you during the second week of your vacation."

I ran over and hugged him. Dad smells very good, like clean, ironed shirts.

I have been on the phone all night.

I talked to Mom. She is coming the first week. Lacey is coming the first week. Howie and the Walkers are coming the second week with Dad-and-April. I said they could bring the dogs.

Saturday, March 6

I am back in school.

Everyone, including Mrs. Prokopovich, acted so happy to see me. She said, "Welcome back, duck!"

Mr. O'Hare is the only one who doesn't seem happy. He is in a very bad mood. Fish told me his mother isn't dating him anymore. Yay! Yay! Mrs. Fisk has come to her senses!

Wednesday, March 17

I am home at Hidden Lake. Mom and I are having such a good time together. Lacey and her father are here, too. Mom and I pretend we are real Yankees, saying "Ayuh," all the time to counteract Lacey's and Mr. Hamilton's "y'alls."

Tuesday, March 23

Dad-and-April are here now. Dad spends a part of each day playing his music. I love the way it sounds. It was snowing outside, and these big fat flakes were coming down. It seemed as if they were falling in time to the music.

It's not exactly spring here, but last week Mom and I put up a few maple syrup buckets; every day now I go out and check them. The sap is running. Spring must be here.

The Walkers are coming tomorrow. It will be fun to have the dogs here.

Guess what? Fish just called and invited himself up. Can you believe the nerve? But you know what? I actually can't wait. I think we are going to have the most fun. There's still a ton of snow up here, and I can't wait to go sledding with him on the big hill.

Thursday, March 25

Fish came up and brought a vanilla-manila envelope with him. "Howie said to give this to you," he said.

I am going to sit under the stairs with Gran's painting of Abby and Biscuit, and read Howie's Silly Wizard story.

Miss Howl, Once an Old Woman

One day Miss Howl had had an especially exhausting day. She had a mountain of papers to correct. She had given her students a great deal of work to keep them quiet. Lately she could not seem to bear the sound of their childish voices.

Normally she loved to correct papers, leaving

little red slashes all over the stupid misspelled words and sloppy punctuation. She liked to write sarcastic comments like, "If this story is based on your real life, then get a different life."

During recess she tried to concentrate, while the high-pitched voices of kids enjoying spring came in the window and grated against her nerves. Here was the childish round girlish script of that not very bright girl Laura (although Miss Howl had to admit Laura had been doing better lately); here was Martin's almost illegible scrawl, little marks like mouse droppings. A strange thought flicked through Miss Howl's mind—what would it be like, she wondered, to eat a mouse, to hear the sound of little bones crunching?

Miss Howl shook herself and pushed the pile of papers away. Perhaps she had been working too hard. She found herself looking out the window, the one that lazy Mr. Old had finally fixed. She saw the boys playing baseball, yelling insults at each other, kicking, hitting, punching, piling on top of each other; the girls huddled in knots, gossiping, giggling, tossing their heads self-consciously. Oh, she loathed kids. Who, in their right minds, would ever choose to be one?

But was it a choice? She frowned. The question had never occurred to her before. Thinking about it made her head ache.

As she continued to look out the window, she realized with a shock that the maple tree that used to be in the middle of the courtyard was no longer there. How long had it been gone? Who had cut it down? She did not know why, but the absence of the tree bothered her deeply.

She scooped up the papers in front of her and tossed them into the wastebasket. "Rubbish," she said to herself. "All rubbish." When the students came back in from recess, she needled the fresh recess health from their cheeks, bored the luster from their eyes, and assigned them all new papers to write.

All that day, her head ached. That night she slept uneasily. Finally, tired of tossing and turning, she sat up in bed and looked out her window. Her eyes adjusted rapidly to the dim outside world, lit wanly by a slim crescent moon. To her surprise Miss Howl was pleased by what she saw.

The shadowy world of night is so much nicer, she thought, than the bright colors of the day. Perhaps she could get Mrs. Morning to have the students come to school at night. Then perhaps she would not feel so irritated.

Oh , why on earth was she teaching? For the second time that day, she realized she didn't like anything about children. She thought of all the hateful things they were. They were noisy. Messy. Dirty.

Rude. Aimless. Clumsy. Thoughtless. Willful. Stubborn. Greedy. Vain. Lazy. Deceitful.

She realized in that moment that she had never had a childhood, so why did anyone else have to have one? And then she blinked her yellow eyes. No childhood? What an odd idea, and oh, how it made her head ache to think such thoughts.

If I wasn't a child, she thought, what was I?

At that moment a tiny but lovely voice floated through the air. It sang a song about forests at night, nests in the tops of trees, and the joys of hunting with talons outspread.

Susan the spider had, after many days of arduous travel, finally climbed into the seventh-grade classroom and swung herself over to Miss Howl and perched, unseen, on her shoulder. She hitched a ride home with Miss Howl. She knew she had a job to do.

Now she was dangling from the ceiling, just an inch or two away from Miss Howl's ear. Miss Howl rose up from her bed as if in a trance. She moved quietly and slowly down the stairs of her house, out the front door, and across her lawn to the rim of the small park across the way.

Miss Howl stepped into a world of tall oaks and pines. An owl hooted above her. Miss Howl closed her eyes and remembered exactly what she had been.

"I am home," she thought. In that moment she

felt again the joy of being a young owl, of waking in her nest with her brothers and sisters, of learning to fly and hunt, of learning to screech. She remembered she had been noisy, messy, and dirty . . . but it was all right to be those things because she was young and she would learn.

Miss Howl opened her eyes and looked up and saw yellow eyes staring back at her. What in the world had led her to be the woman she was now? Tell me, she asked the owl silently. As if the owl could hear her, it screeched; and Miss Howl remembered the night she had flown over the courtyard and had seen the girl laughing and playing beneath her.

Playing . . .

"And I wanted to be one of them," she exclaimed out loud. "So I could play. I asked the Silly Wizard. The Silly Wizard!" She remembered it all now. She was going to have to find that Silly Wizard and give him a piece of her mind.

Miss Howl climbed into her car and drove straight to the school. She marched right to the courtyard where, sure enough, she found Mr. Old. Her yellow eyes were fierce in the moonlight, and Mr. Old found his heart beating quite hard.

"I wanted to be a girl," she said, shaking a bony finger at him.

The Silly Wizard looked at her, quite frightened.

Suddenly he realized there was something different about her. He took a step closer and realized that she didn't look as old as the last time he had seen her. Was he just imagining this? He took one step closer. No, it did seem to be true. And then he understood the silly path his charm had taken.

"You will be a girl," he said. "It's just going to take some time."

"What do you mean?" she asked.

"You are growing backward," he said. "Every year you will be a year younger, and when you get to be school age, you can retire from teaching and become a student. You ought to be very sympathetic toward the teachers, having been one and all."

From that night on, Miss Howl became the best teacher that ever taught at the school. She learned everything she could about childhood from her students. In the meantime she dyed her hair light brown with reddish highlights. She became a very stylish and pretty woman.

Mrs. Morning was very pleased with how things worked out. She prided herself for hiring such a good teacher. Mr. Old was pleased, too. He told himself not to forget again that Silly Wizard magic always does work out, even though it takes its own silly time.

Saturday, March 27

I have a brilliant idea. I am going to put all of Howie's Silly Wizard stories together in one envelope and—no, I can't write it down. If I write down my brilliant idea, it won't come out the way I want it to. I am just going to *do* it; and every time I pass Lizzy in the hallway, I'm going to rub her nose and make a wish.

Tuesday, April 13

I am so busy all the time that I hardly have time to write anymore; but I wanted to say that Howie has started teaching shop, and lots of girls are taking it. He even has a bunch more Silly Wizard apprentices and is assigning them Silly Wizard tasks. I am jealous, but I have to admit I haven't finished mine yet. I still can't crack that A—B—C—D—E WHEEL code.

I am not taking shop because I am playing softball, which I really like. Miss Bean, who is the coach, says I have a wicked good throwing arm.

After school, though, Howie and I have been working on my water clock. It's almost finished. It's not perfect; but there is an Invention Fair this term, and I am going to enter it.

Monday, May 23

Guess what, guess what!

Pocket is having a reunion, and guess who is coming!

Friday, May 28

I hardly write in this diary anymore. I have to admit I used to write more when I wasn't that happy.

But I want to write today because today was the Pocket reunion.

It was funny to see all these older women, walking around, looking at this and that, and saying things like, "Does Miss Hamper still teach here?" or "Oh, I remember this classroom; this is where I failed algebra." They poke their heads into our dorm rooms, and giggle, and say, "This is where Billie, Bugsy, and I roomed together. Bugsy hung on the fire sprinklers and set the sprinklers going, and all the fire trucks came."

They all seem happy to be back and at the same time homesick for when they were young. "You girls look just the way *we* did," they say with a wistful tone in their voices. "The uniforms are a bit different, that's all."

A few months ago I couldn't *imagine* having a homesick feeling about this place. Now just a *tiny* shred of understanding is sneaking in.

They all rub Lizzy's nose when they walk by the mural.

And speaking of Lizzy . . .

During recess I was standing out by the tree, just standing and watching because to tell the truth, having all these strange women visiting was making me feel a bit shy, when I saw Mrs. Walker coming toward me and a tall woman was with her.

The tall woman turned out to be Elizabeth Longford! It took a moment to know who she was, but as I was staring at her, there was this *click* and I suddenly saw her young face inside her old face. It is the *nicest* face, with all these crinkle lines so you know she has laughed a lot, and she still has braids! They are wrapped around her head.

"So nice to meet you, Lydia," she said. "You are Bunny all over again."

She looked around, and put her hand on the tree and said, "You happen to be standing on the only spot that looks as I remember it!"

Fish, Collie, and Lacey came by, and I introduced them. Elizabeth Longford was interested to learn that a boy was going to Pocket. Then the door to Pocket House opened and another oldish woman came out of it. She was wearing a fur coat even though it was pretty warm out, and lots of lipstick and leather gloves. She was carrying a large leather bag. She looked over in our direction and then screamed, "Abby! Lizzy!" And Mrs. Walker and Elizabeth Longford screamed, "Connie!" And then all three of them were laughing and hugging each other. "You look *just* the same!" they were saying to each other.

Connie stepped up to me and said, "And here's Bunny!" I felt a little shiver run down the back of my neck, as if I had turned into my grandmother.

"I'm not Bunny," I said. "I am Lydia Rice, Bunny's granddaughter. I saw one of your pictures in my history text book," I added.

"Well, I've been traveling all day just for this, came all the way from San Francisco to see you, my dear!"

"To see *me?*" I squeaked.

"Abby wrote and told me all about you and absolutely *commanded* me to come out and meet you. And, Lizzy, I want an autographed copy of your latest book. My grandchildren have them all, you know. And when do I get to see Pen? Oh, it's been such a long time, I'm a little afraid to see him, but, oh my goodness, Lizzy and Abby, look at us—we're all so well-preserved, aren't we, as if we haven't aged a day!"

She laughed her head off, and Lizzy said, "Same old Connie." The three of them linked arms, and they all laughed their heads off.

"What a lark!" Connie said. "A reunion! We're almost all still here now, aren't we, the Pocket girls of the mural. You can stand in for Bunny, can't you, Lydia. As for Dorothea—"

"So sad," said Abby.

"He loved her a great deal," said Connie softly.

"A storybook romance," said Lizzy.

"The years go by so quickly, and I was so busy," said Connie. "I meant to keep in touch." She took a huge camera out of her huge bag. "I must capture this moment."

"I'll take it," a deep voice said. We all jumped. We hadn't seen Howie approaching. Everyone seemed to pull in a big breath and then let it out. I wondered if they could see Howie's young face inside his old face. "Hello, Pocket girls," he said. "I'll take the picture. Lydia, you get in that tree."

Everyone laughed as I climbed the tree. I remembered the last time I had been in it and could hardly look at Howie.

There was a lot more laughter and commotion as

they tried to get into the same places they are in the mural—although Elizabeth Longford didn't have a jump rope, Mrs. Walker didn't have a kitten, and Connie wasn't painting. And Dottie wasn't there at all. I guessed everyone was thinking about that, Howie most of all.

When Howie had finished, Connie went over to him, put her arm through his, and said, "I am so sorry about Dorothea; I wish so much she could be here with us." I didn't know what would happen, her saying it out loud like that, but it was amazing. Howie smiled the biggest smile, and even I could suddenly see the young, handsome Mr. Pendragon inside that smile.

"Just your being here makes her seem close by," he said.

"Then we'll have to come more often," said Connie. "We'll come all the time, instead of every forty years or whatever it's been!"

"Come see the old studio," he said to them, and off they went, laughing and talking.

I had to go to history class. I was already wicked late for it. Mr. O'Hare's room was stuffed with old Pocket girls who were visiting classes. He was sickeningly nice all through the class. All the ladies came out of the class exclaiming, "Oh, what a marvelous teacher." I badly wanted to tell them the truth; but, oh well, some truths will never see the light of day.

Later Mrs. Walker said I was invited to come over to

her house after school for a Pocket girl party before they all went back to Pocket for a special reunion dinner. Howie and I were supposed to walk over to her house together. I waited for him outside of Corner House. There is a big lilac bush growing outside the front door, with deep purple flowers, smelling like happiness.

Howie came out. He was all spiffed up. He was wearing a suit. His beard is neat and trimmed now, and he seems more filled out. I think he stands up straighter now than he used to.

"I've never seen you in a suit before," I said. "You look like a penguin. Are you one?"

But Howie didn't smile. He said, "Lydia, I have a bone to pick with you." His voice was gruff, and he looked stern. I felt butterflies in my stomach. What had I done now?

"I gave those Silly Wizard stories to you," he said.

Now the butterflies were big old elephants. I knew where this was headed.

"You sent them to Elizabeth Longford," he said.

I could feel myself blushing. I hung my head. It hit me like a ton of bricks. I had done the wrong thing again. What had I been thinking?

"Elizabeth Longford's publisher wants to publish them. With my paintings."

I squealed and threw myself at Howie. I couldn't help myself. "You're not mad?"

"I should be," he said, "but I'm not." He broke off a little bunch of lilac flowers and handed them to me. "I'm really thankful that you're who you are, Lydia Rice, an impossible, impudent imp."

I carried the flowers all the way to the Walkers, held them the whole time we were there, and carried them back home. They are pressed inside my diary now, and the scent of happiness will stay there forever and ever.

Wednesday, June 2

It is exam time, and school is almost over.

After supper tonight, on my way to study hall, I stopped for a minute on the stairs and looked at the mural.

I looked at Lizzy first and then at Abby, then Dottie, and then Connie. I kept my eyes down on purpose and saved looking at Bunny for last. When I slowly lifted my eyes, what a shock! Bunny was in the tree, grinning away; but poking out of the leaves on the other side is another face! I'm sure it's me!

And then I realized that the whole mural seems spiffed up. I put my hand out and touched it. Sure enough, it has been newly painted! There's even a fresh white P in the bottom corner.

The border is freshly painted, too. The Pocket girls and ABCDE on the left and WHEEL on the right are as bright and clear as they can be.

I jumped back up on the stairs and looked at the whole thing.

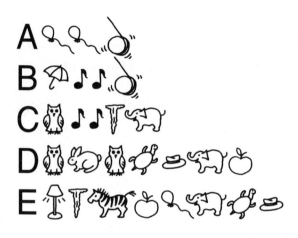

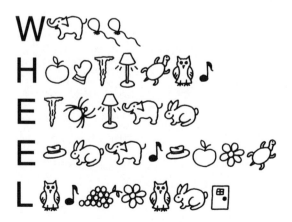

And then my brain went click-click-click, and now I know exactly what ABCDE WHEEL means. I can't imagine what took me so long to figure it out!

"Just what are you doing, lollygagging on the stairs?" Mr. O'Hare was behind me, and he just about startled me out of my skin. "You're going to be late to study hall, Lydia Rice."

"I'm going," I said. I started to skip away.

"What right have you to be so happy?" he growled at me.

"I'm a Silly Wizard," I said. "And I have a charm for everything. What would you like to be, Mr. O'Hare, what would you like to be?"

Letters in code

pp. 145–146
Dear Lacey and Collie,

Meet me in two nights by the tree in the courtyard at 10:30 P.M. for Operation Pig Heart. I have keys. Dress in black and a hat to cover face.

pp. 146–147
Dear Lydia,

I will be there. I don't have anything black. Which hat should I wear? Collie

pp. 147
Dear Lydia,

I don't know. What if we get caught? Lacey

p. 148
Lacey, we won't get caught. I have it all figured out. Be there. L.R.

p. 149
Collie, just wear something to cover up in so you won't be recognized. 10:30. Be there. L.R.

p. 152
Lydia's note: It's off.

Collie's note: How come?

Lydia's note: Can't get the keys.

p. 159
Lydia's note: Operation Pig Heart is on. Have keys. Meet me at 10:30 at the tree Tuesday night.

pp. 215–216
Fish's note: Mr. O'Hare said we shouldn't talk to you. Does what you did have anything to do with keys?

p. 216–217
Mr. O'Hare said we shouldn't talk to you. I think you are very brave. Lacey

p. 217
Here is a candy bar in case you get hungry. Collie

pp. 218–219
Lacey's note: I hope you don't stay up too much longer. I miss you.

pp. 219–220
Fish's note: Here is a sleeping bag. I hope you don't fall out of the tree. If you have to go to the bathroom, my mother is going to leave Corner House unlocked. Fish

p. 249
Abby   Webb
Bunny   Hamilton
Connie   Eisler
Dorothea   Ehrenhaft
Elizabeth   Longford